PAUL ASLING

Bagley's Lane

Blood on the streets

*To my wonderful children, Carly, Leanne and Danny.
I am so proud of you.*

Copyright © Paul Asling 2019

The right of Paul Asling to be identified as the author of this work has been asserted in accordance with the Copyright, Designs & Patents Act 1998.

All rights reserved. No part of this book may be reproduced, stored in a retrieval system, or transmitted in any form or by any means, electronic, electrostatic, magnetic tape, mechanical photocopying, recording or otherwise, without the written permission of the copyright holder.

All characters in this publication are fictitious and any resemblance to real persons, living or dead is purely coincidental.
Published by Independent Publishing

ISBN Number 9781073103263

CHAPTER
1

Having watched her for weeks, he now senses it's time to bring misery and terror to another victim. Craving to see her face and stroke her hair, the hessian sack is still covering her head. Being a stickler for rules, it means the games can't begin. The only sounds he can hear are her sobs and the distant boom of muffled music, coming from a pub nearby. He wants to enjoy this one; he loathed it when they died too soon. Sitting her down on the rubble-laden floor, he rips off the hood and stands back to admire his prey.

Her eyes widen and toxins of terror shoot through her veins. Terrified she screams at the top of her voice, 'Are you crazy? Get away from me.'

Snorting with derision his voice is quiet and calm, 'My love, my mind is clear, I have no madness.'

With adrenaline pumping through him like it's trying to escape from his body, he draws back his right fist and punches her full in the face. The large gold ring on his middle finger, opening up a ragged gash underneath her left eye. Regaining consciousness, she doesn't know how long she'd been out for. The first thing she notices is a copper candlestick, lit with a yellow wax candle, dissipating the surrounding darkness. Breaking the mausoleum-quiet silence, lightning crackles and thunder crashes in the boiling skies above her. Clambering over the rubble to her bag, her heart sinks when she discovers her phones missing. Getting to her feet, a splash of resplendent lightning spotlights a towering figure, emerging from the doorway at the far end of the room. Hearing his ragged gasps, she watches him advancing towards her. Scrambling backwards she comes to a halt against a damp brick wall. Under his cruel, curved bushy eyebrows, his eyes have grown fierce, as insanity has stolen his mind. Inhaling through his nose, he closes his long fingers around the cold handle of the 12-inch knife he's holding. With her screams reverberating through her head, all movement around her has slowed, his voice coming as if underwater. Aside from the beat of her heart, no other muscle in her body is moving. Terrified to the core she longs for the security of home and her dad. Looking at her eyes streaming with tears he knows he should stop; an honourable man would show mercy. But feeling a tremor of euphoria, it exceeds his better nature and spurs him on. The temptation to punish her is poisoning his bloodstream, and he realises he can't stop. Only when she's screaming for mercy, he will finish her. The silver blade squishes home, sending a geyser of blood gushing into the air. Feeling searing pains shooting through her body. Looking down, she sees her blood pulsing in waves. Setting about his task his bloodied fingers curl through her hair, as he licks at her skin with his grainy tongue. Closing her eyes, the picture of him is still there. With her head dizzy and her stomach nauseous, she hears him whispering in her ear, 'I will destroy you, you will be nothing more than blood and bone.'

Her misery is his entertainment. There hadn't been enough in her short life to flash by.

CHAPTER
2

With the broth of summer smells coming in from the garden. DI Luca Rossi is relaxing, reading his newspaper in his sun-drenched kitchen. As the smell of his coffee dissipates into the warm air around him, he's about to phone his brother Franco at the restaurant, when his mobile springs into action. Spotting Sam's name displaying on the blue screen, he knows it will not be good news. Sam and the team know it's a rare day off for him, and it's a year to the day his beautiful wife Julia and children had left.

Lowering his head with irritation, before he can say anything, Sam gets straight to the point, 'Hi boss, I know it's a bad time.'

Luca interrupts, his greeting brief, 'Yes Sam it is, what's up?'

With the tone of his voice not lost on her, Sam tells him, 'An hour ago, a builder phoned in and reported he'd discovered a mutilated body on the building site where he's working. I'm at the scene now; you need to see this boss. I've seen nothing like this in my life.'

'Where are you?'

'The Kensington Olympia end of Holland Park Road.'

'I'll be there in thirty minutes.'

In another life, Luca could have been a male model. He stands over six feet, with a lithe but powerful build. His abundant hair is midnight black and with his eyes a mesmerising brochure blue. He has a face that stops women in their tracks, with many of them doing double takes and being so unassuming with it. It causes women to fall for him regularly. But despite all the opportunities that fall his way, Luca Rossi is a one-woman man. While many of Luca's work colleagues are fashion-phobic, Luca's not. Whatever he's doing, work or social he appears immaculate. And if there's one thing Italian's know, it's everybody looks better in sunglasses, even when it's raining. He's well-read, confident and the accomplished gentleman. His colleague Sam once characterised him as a cross between Harry Potter and a cockney Al Pacino. Standing in the hall, dressed to perfection in his navy blue Canali suit and white shirt, unbuttoned at the collar. He takes his hanky from his pocket and cleans his sunglasses. Perching them onto his nose, he steps back gazing into the gilded hall mirror. Entombed in his thoughts, he has the all too familiar pain, deep in the pit of his stomach. Taking off the sunglasses he sees the hurt reflecting at him in the mirror before him. Only he understands the despair and depression he's burying, from those around him.

A shaft of sunlight is finding its way through the stained-glass window in the front door, hitting a silver-framed photo, standing on the polished veneered table. Peering down, his wife Julia and daughters, Amalee and Darcy are gazing back at him smiling. He misses his girls laughs and the way they'd light up everything around them, even when the sun was burning at its brightest. Smiling back at them, he puts two fingers to his lips and places them onto the photograph.

With misty eyes, sophistication and sureness, he leaves his house in Parsons Green Lane, Fulham at 12.30 pm, and heads to the crime scene. In twenty years of working in the Met Police, he'd seen a lot of things most people would never see in their lives.

He'd thought he'd seen it all, but he was to be wrong, so very wrong.

Sitting at the junction of Dawes Road and North End Road, the roads around him are gridlocked. Watching the shimmering heat lines rising from the scorched bonnet of his dark blue Mercedes, the extreme heat is only being kept in check by the cold breeze, streaming from the air-con vents. North End Road conjures up wonderful memories for Luca. As a young boy, he remembers people packing the market, making it an endless sea of colour and character. The mixture of the smells in the market gave it a unique scent that hung in the air, from early morning to early evening. In those days, you got a dose of local life and access to the freshest and cheapest foods in town. But like many old London markets; North End Road has transformed over the years, in Luca's judgement for the poorer. Back in his childhood, the same families operated the stalls for generations, but now most of the old stallholders had long gone. Luca recalls as a child, market traders lining the full length of North End Road. From Walham Green to Lillie Road, without a single space between them.

The market was a community meeting point for Fulham's old, young, well-off and the struggling. The market had its social code, vocabulary and collective identity. It was vibrant, cheap, rough around the edges but lots of fun. People thrived on interacting with the barrow boys, each one almost a pastiche of effervescent friendliness. He can picture it now, a lost child crying for its mum, a man looking for his dog, stallholders screaming out their offers at the top of their voices to attract customers.

   With sirens and blue lights now flashing, weaving in and out of the traffic Luca hammers his Merc along the busy road. Arriving at the top of North End Road, he screeches right onto Hammersmith Road, thundering past hundreds of people attending the international jewellery show at the Olympia. Luca arrives at Holland Park Road at 1.10 pm and spots the flashing blue lights of two parked police cars.

He brings the Merc to a screeching halt, inches shy of the blue and white tape cordoning off the scene.

CHAPTER
3

The road is affluent and exhibits a stunning terrace of large three million pound plus Georgian houses. Its wideness somehow reminding Luca of walks in the park with his daughters. Rick and Sam spot Luca and stride over to meet him. Taking off his sunglasses he exits the car, with it the sanctuary of the air-con. Sam tells him, 'It's a dreadful one boss. I've seen nothing like it.'

Luca, squinting in the bright sun, asks, 'Male or female?'

Rick exclaims, 'Female. She's not a glamorous sight boss.'

With the afternoon shadows drifting across the road, they head towards the house. Luca can see the property is in a state of renovation from top to bottom. Scaffolding is festooning the four-story home, from top to bottom. The property is a brick skeleton waiting for its restoration. Sitting outside the property is an enormous yellow skip overflowing with builder's rubbish.

In his throaty voice, Rick informs Luca, 'The body's in the basement apartment boss.'

Stopping at the black ornate iron gate leading to the basement. They dress in white protective suits. As they descend the well-worn concrete steps. Adrenaline is flooding Luca's head like it's on an intravenous drip. Entering, the first thing Luca sees a police photographer taking pictures of the scene in meticulous detail. Bloodstains are being recorded, numbered and photographed, the regular drill. The walls of the apartment lay deprived of plaster. Exposing bare red brickwork and dark copper piping. With no ceilings in place, timber joists and metal pipework above are visible. Damp rubble is covering the floor, producing a peculiar musty smell. The echoes of dripping water are coming from the back of the room. An open sewer pipe is also adding to the strange atmosphere.

With building debris crunching under their feet. Sam ushers Luca further into the room. As he enters, darkness closes in around him. Standing in the room's centre, he scans all four corners. To the left of him, a police photographer is stooping down low, snapping away like a beach photographer, at the girl's body. He's concealing the body; all Luca can see at this point are the girl's bare feet and mutilated face. Scrunching his nose, the sweet metallic pungency of the blood is overwhelming his senses and stifling his breathing. The photographer stands aside to allow Luca to get a closer look. She's laid out on the ground like a life-sized doll; her face suspended in a terrified scream. Luca pauses for a few moments without blinking, scrutinising the girl's heinous wounds. The girl resembles a dismembered animal at an abattoir, meat, blood and bones. Luca's mouth is too dry to speak.
In the blistering afternoon heat, the blood has blackened. Making a latticework of crimson threads across her face and chest. Luca spots her clothes and underwear laying to the right-hand side of her body, smothered in blood. Her face is like a disfigured mask, her straight blond hair defiled with blood and gore. The killer has carved her eyelids from her face. Leaving her emerald green eyes wide open. Making them look wild, staring out towards the back garden into the endless blue sky. With her lips have cut from her mouth, its revealing her blood-stained teeth. With her throat cut open wide, Luca can

see her oesophagus and veins hanging from her neck, like a thin red tubing. Even though her throat's slashed, the amount of blood shocks him.
Rick points to her severed body parts, stacked in a neat pile on a builder's saw bench on the far side of the room. The assemblage also includes her tongue.

The photographer asks two of the officers standing nearby to turn the girl's body. Luca had a lot of time for forensic photographers. The job wasn't a walk in the park and required a stomach of steel and the ability to work long, anti-social shifts. The role also required discretion and sensitivity, and the capacity to cooperate with a wide variety of professionals. Including police officers, doctors, lawyers and court officials.
Her legs are apart; her left leg is straight, her right leg bent at the hip and knee. Her left arms curled under her body, her right hand four inches from her face. Luca notes rigor mortis is clear.
Two officers turn the girl and find the back of her skull smashed open. Parts of her brain now blended with the sand and rubble on the floor. The carnage is indescribable as he undertakes to detach himself from the overwhelming scene in front of him. A lone drop of sweat makes its way down his back, leaving a trail of temporary coolness in its wake.

   He tells Rick, 'It's obvious the slaughter's taken place here.'

   Rick growls, 'I can't help wondering how much of the process she lived through.'

   Rick's comment sends a cold shiver down Sam's spine.

   Luca ponders, 'There's no sign of a gag. I bet he enjoyed her screams. If he did, it won't be his last victim.'

Sam asks Luca, 'Have you seen anything like this before boss?'

Luca shakes his head and sighs, 'No, not on this scale.'

Kneeling, Luca detects the whiff of sweat and leather mixed with blood as he reaches out to the girl's bag. Frowning with concentration, with the tip of his pen he pulls apart the top of the dark brown leather bag. Picking up a red plastic credit card holder on the top of the bag's contents. He stands and opens it, finding her work ID and two credit cards. Inspecting the work pass; it displays a photo; her name is Carol Lane, and she's nineteen years old. Further scrutiny reveals her address, Tadema Road, Chelsea. The work pass also shows she worked for a bank in Canary Wharf.

Dominated by a profound sadness, Luca is standing by the door that leads to the small garden. Breaking the silence, Sam asks, 'Do these bastards get a buzz when their victims cry for mercy. What the hell drives them to this?'

Luca muses, 'Nobody knows the answer to that question Sam. Every killer and every killing is unique. Lust killers, derive erotic gratification from killing. Thrill killers, get a kick from it. Gain killers, murder because they believe they will profit. Power killers wish to play God, to be in charge of life and death.'

He adds, 'I'll leave it to you and Rick to secure the scene. If you find anything significant, can you let me know? Before the end of the day, get what information you can on the girl's parents and siblings. Also, check to see if she had a partner. Can you tell the doctor to get his initial report to me, first thing tomorrow morning? And arrange a briefing with the team tomorrow at 7.30 am? I want everyone there, without fail.'

'One more thing Sam, I don't want the press to get hold of this, not yet anyway.'

Leaving the grim, depressing scene. He heads to South Kensington to meet his brother Franco at the family restaurant as arranged. Driving along Kensington High Street, he still has the horrific images of the girl fresh in his mind. He knows this murder is different and the killings have only begun. Over the years, Luca had often found himself in positions where he saved people's lives. Every fight he broke up, every incident of domestic violence he responded to. May have been a fatality in the making before he prevented it.

Now at this level in his career, one day he could investigate a double murder, the next day, capturing high-profile drug dealers. No two days were ever the same. For him, there wasn't anything more rewarding than stopping a crime in progress. Or arresting a person who had victimised an innocent person.

Whenever he told someone he was a police officer, they'd say something to the effect of, 'I don't know how you do it.'

It was days like today he understood why a lot of police officers liked a drink. But the days are long gone when you would find a bottle of whiskey in the DI's bottom drawer. Alcohol flowed off-duty these days. Within reason, Luca didn't mind his team having a drink. He saw it as an opportunity for the team to unwind after a long stressful shift. For some officer's it's a way of deadening the senses at the end of a challenging day, precisely what he's feeling now.

He knew he was a useless drinker, with no capacity for the stuff, two pints about his limit. But he loved the company of his colleagues, and they liked his. On occasions, after a long shift, the team would go for a pint or two at Smithfield Market. Sometimes after a lot of persuading, he'd agree to join them. But he could never get used to it. It seemed weird to him, drinking beer at the start of a day, then stuffing himself with a full English breakfast.

Not sure how much sleep he will get tonight, before tomorrow's briefing. There are too many images jostling through his mind. But he knew it was all part of the job. His thoughts turning to the dead girl's family; he couldn't comprehend what they are about to go through.

CHAPTER
4

Luca arrives at the family restaurant in Harrington Road, South Kensington at 3.30 pm. The gold letters of the restaurant's name 'Gianni's' are shimmering in the afternoon sunshine. Against its royal blue background. A chalky white line of a passenger jet trails above in the stark blue sky, away from the harsh orange sun. It appears thousands of Japanese tourists are thronging the sun-infused pavements. Taking photos of everything that moves. Taking a deep breath, he enters the restaurant. The air in the restaurant is more delicious than any flavour on offer. The distillation of smells is capturing everything good; coffee, cured meats, focaccia, baked lasagne and the gutsy aroma of red Italian wine. The fragrance that's dissipating into the warm air is intoxicating. Taking Luca straight back to his childhood.

Gianni's is large yet cosy. With its bright lights and colourful walls, its interior is warm and cheery. The layout is simple, a counter covering the entire length of the right-hand side wall. In front, tables are set out with sparkling cutlery and glasses and rolled white napkins. To the left side is a wide ornate wooden staircase, leading to more tables and balcony area. Overlooking Harrington Road. The restaurant is full. A young couple are sitting side-by-side tucking into their garlic bread. A group of women in their thirties are laughing and giggling, each holding a large glass of red wine. Luca's brother Franco is standing behind the counter, making a cappuccino for a customer and doesn't see Luca enter. His sister Martina is chatting and laughing with four businessmen in dark suits, sitting at a table at the back. It's business as usual.

Luca was born in Hammersmith Hospital in the summer of 1972. His parents Gianni and Rosa had left Sorrento, Italy to live in London in 1961. Gianni's older brother Antonio, already living in London, owned the restaurant. Gianni and Rosa settled quickly, renting a flat in William Parnell House, in the Bagleys Lane area of Fulham. In 1970, Antonio had a massive heart attack and died. Luca's father Gianni then inherited the restaurant outright. When Gianni died in 1995 after a short illness. Luca, Franco and Martina inherited the restaurant on his death.

Luca visits the restaurant most days, but on this visit a better sight awaited him. Marie, the head waitress appears at the top of the stairs. Descending her skirt is billowing around her. Marie is beautiful in the classical sense; there's something about her that makes her irresistible. Marie's hair is long, straight and black. Her eyes are dark liquid pools. With her breasts high and full, it gives her the perfect hourglass figure. Her ebony eyes light up like a Christmas tree when she spots Luca standing in the central part of the restaurant. Since his separation from Julia, she flirts
with him at every opportunity. When she gets to the bottom of the stairs, she stands with her right hip jutted to one side, and her right arm draped in front embracing her left elbow. With her dark hair laying on her shoulders like a flowing black waterfall. She asks, 'Hi, how's my favourite boss today?' Her rich Italian accent saucy and provocative.

With a wide grin. He tells her, 'I'm fine Marie, and you look as gorgeous as ever.' She smiles and offers to make him a coffee. He accepts and heads for the kitchen. The assistant chef greets him and makes room at a small table in the kitchen's corner. Sitting down he notices a man coming out of the cellar entrance. The man has a mop in one hand and a bucket of soapy water in the other. He's tall, spindly and dressed in brown overalls. His greasy brown hair slicked back and is receding like a pond that's drying up fast. He has strange birded-like features, a beaky nose and squinty eyes, set deep into his skull.

Marie approaches, 'Here you go boss, one special cappuccino.'

'Who's the man going out into the backyard?'

'That's Reg, our new handyman; he started two weeks ago. He comes in four days a week to clean the yard, cellar and drains. His main job is across the road at the Victoria and Albert Museum. Why do you ask?'

'Nothing, he looks odd, that's all.'

'I know what you mean, he gives me the creeps, but he's a nice man once you get to know him.'

Sipping his coffee his mind wanders to Julia and the children, and what had happened one year ago today. His chest aches as he thinks of what he's lost. No one had replaced her, and he knew no one ever could. Daily he puts on a feigned smile, to mask his pain from his family and friends. But the pain is becoming all too unbearable. It hurts now even to fake his smile.

He jumps when from behind his sister Martina taps him on the shoulder. Rising to his feet, he kisses her on both cheeks.

Sitting down opposite him with her coffee, she looks him straight in the eyes, 'I can see your heart is breaking, the year has passed so fast.'

With sadness in his dark eyes, he replies, 'It never goes away sis; I miss them so much. As mum used to say, it seems sadness is my best friend at the moment.'

With her eyes locked on him, she asks, 'What are you doing tomorrow evening?'

Shaking his head, he smiles, 'Well, put it this way sis, I am not in the mood for clubbing, what have you got in mind?'

She laughs, 'A charity dinner at the V&A Museum. I have three tickets. I thought you me and Marie, what do you think?'

Finishing his coffee, he jests, 'Not seeking to match us up are you, sis?'

'No, of course not. Would I do such a thing?'

'How did you get your hands on the tickets?'

'From a guy, I've been seeing over the last few months.'

'Yes, that's fine, I could do with a night out, I've not had one in ages. Is it black tie?'

'Yes, and I want to see you in all your finery. I will let Marie know, shall we meet here at 7.30 pm?'

'See you tomorrow sis.

Getting up, he leaves the kitchen to find Franco. Franco sees him entering and greets him with a hug, enquiring, 'How is it going big guy; I haven't seen you for a few days?'

'I'm fine, who's this guy Martina's been seeing?'

Franco smiles, amused, 'She's told you then? His name is Albert Mason, have you heard of him? She tells me he's well known in the City.'

Luca thinking for a few seconds, 'Yes, I have if it's the same one. He's a well-known businessman from Fulham with a big reputation.'

Franco asks, 'Good or bad?'

Luca frowns, 'Depends on who you are speaking to.'

Franco, grimacing adds, 'I'm only interested in the bad bits brother.

'He's a womaniser, ruthless businessman and has connections with various criminal gangs all over London. And as you said, he's well known in the City of London. As a shark of the highest order.'

Franco shakes his head, and a look of disdain flashes across his face, 'Fucking hell, nice one sis.'

'You may not remember, but his family lived in Bagleys Lane when we lived in William Parnell House with mum and dad.

Franco responds, 'I remember him; he was a huge kid, always fighting. He always seemed to wear baggy jumpers with holes in. Didn't he live with his mother and brother? His father committed suicide when the boys were young.'

'I'm uncertain about the suicide, but I'll let you know more. It looks like I will be meeting him at the V&A charity event, tomorrow night.'

CHAPTER
5

At forty-nine, Franco is the eldest of the three siblings. He doesn't have the looks of Luca or Martina but has a good business brain. To his friends and family, he's known as Bull. He's huge, strong and not afraid of anybody or anything. Married to a local girl Lisa, they have no children and live above the restaurant. Fearless in everything he undertakes in life he's always looked out for Luca and Martina. Franco's eyes are a well of jet black, and he has a gaze, more fearsome than an agitated lion. He's a fighter, never questioning, always courageous. Standing six feet three, he has shoulders which look as though they could span the Thames. Although he looked tough, he could be a real softy. His full mouth curves downwards at the corners and gives him an expression intended to be stern, but only makes him look kind. He's a man you never tired of, he's funny, smart, witty and is the life and sole of any place he inhabits. To his family, Franco is dependable and warm, but if anybody crossed him or his family, then God help them.

Luca knew of Franco's connections with various other London based Italian families, but they never debated it. Since a child, Franco had always chosen to face fear and conquer it. His attitude in life was simple if you didn't face fear, how else were you going to make progress in life?

Leaving the restaurant, Luca heads off towards Fulham. Since Julia and the children had left, he feels like someone has stabbed him in the heart a thousand times, without dying. His suffering comes in quiet moments when driving, or he's about to sleep. Reaching Fulham Broadway, his eyes become glazed with tears. He'd been holding in his emotions in for months. He blinks, and a tear drops from his eye and slides down his cheek. He hates being unhappy and keeping it bottled up inside, especially from his family. He contemplates going to see Julia unannounced, there and then. But like many times before, he decides against it. Driving along Fulham Road, Luca remembers he should have spoken to his governor, about Rick's promotion prospects. He met Rick at the met police training centre over 15 years ago and remained friends ever since. Rick's been supportive as a colleague and a good friend over the last twelve months, and they've grown even closer.

Born in Queen Charlotte's Hospital and brought up in Pimlico. He boxed from the age of twelve for the Westminster Amateur Boxing Club and was three times a London Schoolboy Champion. Competing twice for England, in his ten years of boxing, he gained over 40 medals and trophies. Married to Marilyn, the couple have three children and live in West Kensington. An old-fashioned policeman, he believes officers should police the streets, and not stuck behind their desks. He's tough but fair and funny with it. A real bruiser of a man, but now in his mid-forties is not so quick on his feet. Luca's told him on many occasions, he moved as fast as a falling brick wall. Whenever Rick spoke, every head in the room turned.

He had such a booming voice he made Brian Blessed sound like a little girl. When Luca reaches home, gloomy-looking clouds have blackened the sky.

He enters and like his life at the moment; the house is empty. He's supposed to feel happy coming to a place where he expects to have peace, love, and contentment. But he feels lonely, and it's leaving him tired, rundown and hollow.

The next morning, Luca's startled when Classic FM booms into life from his alarm clock at the side of his bed. Dressed in blue pyjama bottoms and a white T-shirt, he heads for the kitchen and the kettle. Gazing into the garden waiting for the kettle to boil, his mobile phone bleeps, it's a text from Julia. His brows lower in concentration as he grasps the phone. He holds his breath and senses a flutter in his stomach, but she's only asking him if he's still ok to have the girls at the weekend. It's a text, but it gives him a pleasant feeling inside. Since they broke up, they've only communicated by text or through the girls. He still clings to the belief, she will not ask for a divorce and he feels without this request there is still hope. He still thinks in his heart; it will all be ok, and they would reunite forever.

Leaving the house at 7 am he arrives at headquarters half an hour later. After a brief hello to the uniformed officers chatting at the front desk. He steps into the incident room, the fragrance of sweating bodies hitting him. Pacing across the floor, he opens the windows; the fresh air is like a soft, cool stroke across his face. The room is a large open-plan office. Mugshots and crime scene pictures adorn the walls, and witness statements litter the desks. He can see the team have toiled hard and long into the night.

He bellows across the crowded room, 'Listen up, can we have hush please, we have work to do.' There's immediate silence.

'Rick, can you start us off?'

Rick's voice reverberates around the room, 'As you know the murdered girl is a nineteen-year-old Carol Lane. She lived in Tadema Road, Chelsea. Building contractor, Frank Ives found her at 11 am yesterday morning in Holland Park Road. When he opened up the site. We've questioned him, and he has a solid alibi, for the estimated time of the victim's death. For the present time, we've excluded him from our investigations. No other builders we know of, have been on site since last Monday. They've all been working on another site in Fulham Palace Road. We are looking at their whereabouts, at the estimated time of the girl's murder.

Scratching his jaw, Rick clears his throat and moves on, 'The girl was wearing a white sleeveless blouse and short navy-blue skirt. Her jewellery included two small gold hoop pierced earrings and a gold chain bracelet. Her killer left her jewellery, cash, credit cards, clothes and underwear at the scene, along with her brown leather handbag. We didn't find her mobile phone at the scene. Preliminary indicators, including body temperature and rigor mortis. Estimate her time of death, between 11.30 pm on Wednesday 30th July and 6.30 am on Thursday 31st July subject to review, pending the formal autopsy. Sam takes over, a twinge of anger lacing her voice, 'The initial examination of the pelvic area showed the victim had never given birth and was not pregnant at the time of death. The examination showed her killer had snapped her hyoid bone. The killer also severed her tongue, lips and eyelids, stacking her severed body parts in a neat pile on a builder's saw bench, at the scene. Her fingernails were broken. We assume by her clawing at the floor struggling to escape her killer.'

With an uneasy stance, one of the officer's interrupts, 'What the hell is the hyoid bone?'

Luca responds, 'It serves as an anchoring structure for the tongue. The bone is at the root of the tongue in the neck's front, between the lower jaws.'

Shaking his head and a sigh escaping his lips, the officer responds, 'This has got to be one sick bastard.'

Sam carries on, 'Also mentioned in the report was an upward-angled ligature mark on the upper neck of the victim. Consistent with the belt found next to her.

Rick interjects, 'Her assailant beat her about the face, breaking her nose and both cheekbones. The killer also shattered her skull at the rear, leaving her brain visible. The examination also revealed rectal tearing and bite marks on her left breast.'

Silence seeps into the room like a poison paralysing the team from either speech or movement. They stand opened mouthed, eyes wide, perturbed at what they're hearing.

Luca stands, peering into their eyes which are burning with anger. He breaks the silence and asks, 'Have we made all house-to-house enquiries?'

Sam assures him, 'It's ongoing boss, but nothing of significance yet.'

Luca asks, 'Who's spoken to her family?'

Rick states, 'Sam and I spoke to her father yesterday afternoon when we broke the news to him. Her mother died two years ago from breast cancer.'

'Sam, arrange another meeting with the father later today; I will go with you.'

'Rick, can you get someone to check out all CCTV in the area?'

'I'm on it, boss. We've pulled all CCTV from the surrounding area and have three of the team going through it.'

Luca asks Sam, 'Have we put a trace on her mobile?'

'Again, we are on it.'

Luca concedes, 'This is bad, the worst I've seen. We need to find this bastard and quick. You know what to do; so, let's get on with it.'

'Oh, one more thing Sam, can you get a family liaison officer sorted?'

'Already done boss.'

CHAPTER
6

Driving through the busy Kings Road on the way to meet Carol Lane's father.

Sam enquires, 'Have you got the children staying over this weekend?'

'No, I've put them off again because of this mess. Julia's not a happy person, and I don't blame her. I'm about as attractive as root canal treatment at the moment. I've told her I would have them next weekend.'

He adds, 'Newcomers to this job should sign a bloody statement, acknowledging it will guarantee them a divorce.'

Luca believed two main factors caused his marriage breakdown. The stress of the job contributed to destabilising his marriage with Julia. The second reason being, the working of long, unsociable hours. He was rarely at home at nights to help with the children, and rarely around to spend quality time with his family, including the weekends.

Luca loves the Kings Road, but in his eyes, it's changed a lot from the 1960s, 70s and 80s. When along with Carnaby Street, it was the centre of all things fashion in London. It's now a multi-cultural melting pot of the rich and not-so-rich. In past days, it had the prominence of a shopping mecca. But is now home too many of the same shops found on other British high streets, such as Marks and Spencer and McDonald's. Turning left into Tadema Road, the Lots Road Power Station looms up at the side, like a colossal red bricked fortress. Halfway up on the left-hand side of the tree-lined road, they find Robert Lane's house. The white three-storey property has sashed bay windows and black iron railings adorning the front.

Luca knew full well losing a loved one through murder was the most traumatic experience anyone could face in their life. It's an event for which no one can prepare for and leaves in its wake tremendous emotional pain and upheaval. When there's a murder, it's immediate, and it's inconceivable for those left behind. Their loved one is no longer there, and any plans are no longer possible and gone forever. Murder creates overwhelming grief for the family. Their world's turned upside down, and nothing in life prepares them for the reality that someone they love has died a violent death. It results in the survivors grieving not only the person but how the person died. When the life of the victim's cut short, through an act of cruelty. The disregard for human life adds overwhelming feelings of turmoil, injustice and helplessness, to the usual sense of loss and sorrow. The shock of losing someone to murder takes hold immediately and leaves family members shocked and perplexed.

With great trepidation, they climb the three steps to the front door, and Sam presses the
doorbell. The door swings open and Robert Lane pokes out his head. He looks to be in his late forties. He has curly light-brown hair, brown eyes and bushy eyebrows. With his face furrowed and his mouth set in a hard line, he gestures for them to enter. Distraught he leads them into the lounge, his shoulders drooped and gait slow. Luca and Sam offer their condolences.

With sunlight illuminating the room, pictures of Robert, his deceased wife and his murdered daughter Carol, are adorning the white-painted walls. A tan-coloured sofa stands along one wall with two oak tables on either side.

A lamp sat on each table. Robert has the look of a man caught in the road's middle, and a big red number eleven bus bearing down on him.

He looks at Luca, swallowing hard, and asks, 'Have you any more news?'

Shaking his head, Luca reports, 'No, nothing more than you already know Mr Lane.'

Crestfallen, Robert's hands shake. His eyes shift to one side, becoming glazed with tears. Blinking, his tears drip from his eyes and slide down both cheeks. Biting his lip, he tries to hide the sounds that are trying to escape from his mouth.

Luca enquires, 'When did you last speak to Carol?'

With his voice breaking with emotion he replies, 'At 6 pm on Wednesday. She told me she was meeting friends in a pub in South Kensington, then going for a meal.'

'What route would she have taken, did she drive?'

'She would have taken the bus; she doesn't drive. I've recently been teaching her. She had her test booked for next week.' Robert breaks down, sobbing his heart out.

Putting her hand on his shoulder, Sam asks, 'Can I make you a cup of tea Mr Lane?' Robert sniffs, nods and points to the kitchen.

He tells Luca, 'Carol was the only thing left in my life. My wife Susan died of breast cancer two years ago; my daughter was all I had left in the world. I loved her so much. I used to think of her as a flower waiting to bloom. Now it will never happen.'

Luca probes, 'Where was Carol meeting her friends and at what time?'

'She told me she was meeting them in the Six Bells pub Gloucester Road, at seven, and would be back by eleven. I don't know where they were going for a meal.'

Sam re-enters the room and hands Robert his tea and asks, 'How long had Carol worked at the St James Bank, Mr Lane?'

'She'd been working there for the last two years. Some days we would meet for lunch. I run a property investment company in Canary Wharf, two minutes from her office.'

Luca asks, 'Did Carol have a boyfriend or partner, Mr Lane?'

'No, not that I know of, when can I see, her?'

Luca tells him, 'No one should tell a father he should not to see his daughter's body, Mr Lane. Here, we suggest you don't.'

The scene is heartbreaking, Robert puts his face down into his hands, and looks back up at Luca. Tears race down his cheeks, like water from a dam, dripping from his wobbling chin. He's unable to speak, unable to breathe; his sobs are resonating throughout the house.

'I want to kiss her one last time. I loved her so much; she was my little girl. I keep asking myself over and over; what did she go through? Why wasn't I there to protect her?'

Sam, trying to change the subject, asks, 'What was Carol like as a person?'

'Carol had so many of her mother's traits and idiosyncrasies. She was fearless, funny and generous. To be in her company made you feel special. There was nothing I wouldn't have done to keep her safe from harm. But I knew I couldn't always be there to protect her. My daughter saw excitement and promises. As a father, I saw a world of danger and uncertainty.'

Luca asks, 'Could we have a look in Carol's bedroom?'
Robert nods. They both stand and head to her room, their steps sounding hollow on the wooden stairs.
Carol's room is at the rear of the house, on the first floor. The room is serene and painted pastel blue, which seems to make it pulse in the light. It contains a single bed and two dark blue straight-backed chairs. On two of the walls are black and white photographs of Carol as a child with her mother and father. A small window looks out onto the back garden, where a fly is buzzing, trying to get out. Sam studies a chalkboard that's tacked on to the back of the door, plastered with personal messages from Carol to herself. But none are of any significance.
Spotting a photograph album on a table beside the bed, Luca flicks through a montage of Carol's life. Starting with pictures of her as a baby girl, then a toddler, giving way to a tiny schoolgirl. Finally, a blossoming adolescent and a beautiful young woman.
Taking Carol's laptop from the room, Sam follows Luca downstairs. Entering the living room, they can see Robert has calmed down, 'Did you find anything?'

Sam replies, 'No we haven't Mr Lane. Our forensic team will be with you later. We need to take Carol's laptop with us now though.'

Robert muses, 'Often the stronger the parental bond, the harder the teenage years are for a child. They seek to break free, but Carol was different. We stayed close in her teenage years. Believe me; a daughter is a precious gift.'

Luca thinks of his daughters, smiles and says nothing.

When they get back to the car, Luca tells Sam, 'I feel so sorry for him. Where parents cannot view their loved one's body, it's often difficult for them to accept the reality of their loved one's death. But with the mess she's in, as painful as it may be for him, we can't let him see her.' Sam nods in agreement.

He tells Sam, 'When we get back, go over to her workplace in Canary Wharf and see what you can find out. I will talk to Rick and ask him to find out more about Robert Lane and his business?'

CHAPTER
7

Getting ready for the charity event at the V&A Luca's thoughts turn to Julia. He met her on a pleasant summer's evening in August 1998, at the White Horse Pub in Parsons Green. On that hot balmy night, the sun was still casting its golden rays and brushing the sky shades of red and pink, when he arrived at the pub with his friend Steve. They grabbed two lagers and sat outside in the beer garden, which overlooked Parson's Green. Despite being only 7 pm, loud music is coming from inside — the music that's played a little too loud for the neighbours liking. Sitting in the early evening sunshine, Luca hears giggling and the sound of glass on glass. Glancing over to his right, he spots two girls sitting at the table beside him stirring cocktails. One girl meets his gaze and smiles at him. Following suit, he then looks away. After ten minutes, looking over again, he sees the girls getting their things together, to leave. As they walk by before he can stop himself, he asks, 'Where are you two off to then?' Forever reserved and shy, it was not his style.

   The girls stop in their tracks and glare at him. He stammers for a moment but notices warm smiles on their cheerful cheeks, which immediately puts him at ease. He was so shy as a young boy; he'd hide behind his mother, using her as a shield, between her and any stranger. As a teenager with girls, he would let his friends do the talking, as he would blush and get his words mixed up. It seemed the two girls were staring at him for ages. When he tried to speak, it seemed he had a mouthful of sawdust.

Steve returning from the loo, jumps in and takes over, 'What would you, beautiful girl's like to drink?'
The girls look at each other, giggling. Taking their orders, he heads back to the bar, leaving Luca alone with the girls, scurrying to get rid of the clutter from the seat next to him. The girl that sits down beside him can't be over eighteen or nineteen. Her name is Julia. Her voice is warm and rich. Dressed casual but smart, in a white shirt and faded blue jeans which mould around her hips and thighs. Freckles lay over her nose and upper cheeks, and her long golden hair flows halfway down her back. She has delicate carved facial bones, perfect lips and the body of a well-toned ballerina.
Later in the evening, Steve leaves with the other girl, Suzanne, to get a bite to eat. Luca and Julia stay sitting in the warm summer air chatting until last orders. Earlier in the evening, she'd told him she lived in the Worlds End area of Chelsea. When the bell sounds for final orders, being the
perfect gentlemen he asks to take her home, and she agrees. The night is still warm, so they walk. Strolling along the New Kings Road by Eel Brook Common, the silver moon is spilling from the inky black cloudless sky, silhouetting the trees. They sit down on a wrought-iron bench chatting in the moonlight.

Julia seemed to laugh most of the way home that night. At one point she tells him, drying her eyes, 'Stop it, or I'll wet myself.' He found her laugh infectious.

On reaching Julia's flat in Hazlebury Road, they sit on the concrete steps that lead up to the front door. Sitting chatting like they'd known each other for years, not a few hours ago, Luca doesn't want the night to come to
an end. But they say their goodbyes and agree to meet the next night and go for a drink.

On the way home, he thinks about his life and where it's going. He'd had plenty of girlfriends, but none of them lasted for more than a few weeks. It was down to him; he loved his freedom and had no intention of becoming tied down, with anyone. His dream is to work in Italy for two years and meet his extensive family. But tonight, he felt excited, and it would be the start of a journey, neither of them would ever forget.

CHAPTER 8

Arriving at Gianni's at 7.30 pm to meet Martina and Marie, the bouquet of the many restaurants in the area mingle into one. The air is warm, and the rich golden sun is descending into the blue sky of West London. Spotting Martina and Marie standing outside the entrance, posing like models, in their elegant black dresses. He tells them, 'You both look amazing.'

Marie gives a bold smile, 'You don't look bad yourself, boss.'

Martina declares, 'It's a glorious evening, lets walk?'

Reaching Cromwell Road two minutes later, they cross the busy road. Smiling to himself, he recalls a London cab driver once describing the Cromwell Road as the road to hell. The great gothic magnificence of the V&A building rises in front. The elegant architecture still amazes him even though he passes it every day. He recalls going to the museums in the area, on Sunday afternoons in his teenage years with his mates. Not to look at the exhibits but to chat up girls, who also hung around there. Arriving at the main entrance, he spots the spindly figure of Reg the restaurant's handyman, entering a side entrance. But doesn't mention it to the girls. Black taxi's and luxurious cars are queuing around the circular entrance, in front of the imposing building. Entering the magnificent hall, they're presented with a glass of Champagne. Representatives from City banks and other firms based in the London area, along with famous dignitaries. Including the Mayor of London, are filling the place to its rafters. Smiling, Luca watches

Marie scrutinising the host of luxury items the museum will auction throughout the night.
The lights are bright, and a traditional jazz band is playing in the corner of the hall. With guests announced on arrival, Luca can hear the clacking of high heels, echoing across the marble floor. A blend of perfume, polish and candles hit their nostrils, as the three of them stand and chat, sipping their Champagne, surrounded by the other guests.

Luca spots a tall man dressed in a white dinner jacket and red bow tie approach. He appears to be in his mid-fifties and towers above everybody in the room. The man tugs at the starched sleeves of his shirt cuffs, straightens his jacket and stops in front. Martina smiles and puts out her arms, 'Albert, how are you?'

A smile spreads across Albert's face but doesn't make it to his eyes. Stooping down, he kisses Martina on both cheeks. Martina introduces him to Luca and Marie, and they exchange pleasantries. Albert declares, 'You are all sitting at my table for dinner; follow me.

Wandering to the dining room, Albert's shaking hands with what seems like every person in the room, including the Mayor of London. It appears everyone knows Albert Mason.
The dining room is festooned with silver and gold wallpaper and substantial gilt mirrors adorn the walls. The ceiling is at least thirty feet high and white plaster mouldings of exotic fruits and flowers, are gracing its edges. In the ceiling's centre is a large, ostentatious chandelier, which is glaring down onto the guests below. On the dining tables, tall silver candelabras hold long white candles that command attention, from the centres. Flickering, the candles are making ghostly figures dance

across the walls. The polished silverware is heavy to the hand and is twinkling in the soft light.

Luca, who is sitting opposite Albert, notices the candlelight making his face look mysterious. Albert is an imposing six-foot-eight and well-built. His hair is short, dyed black and going into middle-age retreat. His dark eyebrows slope down with intensity, and his nose ended blunt, rather than a point. His face looks like it's fashioned from granite, making it look like it held many secrets.

After dinner, Albert is looking confident, as though he owned the place. He's standing in the middle of a group of backslapping sycophantic guests. Luca watches him shaking hands and schmoozing with everybody around him. Albert knows how to work the room and it seems the guests have many questions.

Taking a hanky from the inside his jacket pocket, Luca polishes his glasses and makes a beeline for Albert, 'My sister has told me so much about you Albert.'

Glancing at the other guests around him, Albert responds 'All good I hope?'

'Mostly.'

'What business are you in Luca?'

Getting straight to the point, Luca tells him, 'I'm a DI in the Met.'

Albert's startled and Luca can see he's lost his initial enthusiasm.

Albert's face drains with a gaunt expressionless stare, 'Interesting, I've many friends in the force.'

Luca thinks to himself 'I bet you have.'

'You must know all that's going on, in the London business world Albert?'

Albert leans forward, whispering, 'I know all, my friend.'

Luca enquires, 'I remember your family, you have a brother, don't you?'

'Yes, how do you know?'

'My family lived near you many years ago.'

'Where was that?'

'My family lived in William Parnell House when you lived in Bagleys Lane.'

'How strange, your right, but I don't recall you or your family.'

A sudden smack of hard light hits Albert's face, which makes him look strange. His eyes become dull and dark. Looming over Luca with eyes of strength and power, 'Well it's nice chatting with you Luca, we must get together sometime soon.'

It seems Albert Mason can't wait to get away. As he leaves, he introduces Luca to a woman who's been standing near them, earwigging the whole conversation. He watches Albert pacing across the room in even strides, with the stiffness of a Sergeant Major, a clear head higher than everybody else in the room, heading for the podgy fair-haired figure of the Mayor of London. The woman who Luca's now talking to has the face of a withered clown balloon. Listening to her droning on about how precious and connected she's boring him rigid. Making his excuses, he leaves the woman standing alone. Martina who had been watching Luca and Albert chatting, approaches, with Marie in tow.

Smiling, she asks 'What do you think of him then?'

Luca not giving anything away, and feeling deep down that Albert is a complete wrong un.

Declares, 'Yes, an interesting guy, sis.'

Marie butts in, 'His eyes are cold.'

Martina replies, 'I used to think his blue eyes were cold too. But now I know the fiercest fires burn blue.'

People in the room turn and stare as Marie laughs hysterically. The laugh reverberating across the room.

Luca spots a woman sitting to the side of him scanning the room with determination, looking like she's in search of someone. When their eyes meet, he smiles at her. With his smile registering with her, she smiles back, her emotions not hidden. Raising her chin, she smiles at him again.

Taking a sip of his drink, he approaches, 'You look like you've lost someone?'

Raising his glass, he asks, 'Another one?'

'A Prosecco would be nice, thanks.'

Standing at the bar, the woman's low-cut dress his hanging from her shoulders, hugging her form. Staring at him, her eyes are sharp and assessing. Over the woman's shoulder, Luca spots Martina looking over at him, grinning from ear to ear. Giving her a wave followed by a cheeky grin, she rolls her eyes at him. The woman standing next to him could have decorated any magazine cover. There's a coyness to her and a warmth in her voice. Her eyes are sparkling blue, and her blond hair is cascading down her back, like a glorious waterfall. She has cherry lips and crystal white teeth. She's a beautiful sight.

Having been in this situation many times since the break-up, he knows nothing will come of it. Feeling alone and isolated, he hears Julia's voice in his head; he recalls the silly things she used to say and the love she gave him. He attempts to throw it out of his head but the guilt and his love for her, keep coming. Julia torments him in ways he could never describe. When the guilt came, it took him down the old familiar path. He wants to refuse to walk it, but he can't. People around him think he's happy, but they don't understand. His panic kicks in and he feels his chest tighten. As if his muscles are deciding not to let another breath into his body. Making his excuses, he heads for the shelter of Martina and Marie.

CHAPTER
9

Albert William Mason was born in a modest terraced house in Bagleys Lane, Fulham in June 1960. When his father committed suicide, his mother Florence received the sum of ten shillings per week widow's pension. Times were harsh, and she took on three jobs to keep the family fed and housed. Albert's recollections of growing up in Fulham in the 60s and 70s included a tin bath, filled with the kettle and saucepans every Friday night. In the long dark months of winter, he recalls the general tepidness of the bath water, leaving him shaking and blue. Sharing a small bedroom with his brother Jack, there was no heating in the house, apart from a smelly paraffin heater. It was so cold the brothers would huddle up together under blankets and coats, that Florence had spread over the bed. Sometimes even that didn't warm them in the colder months. Britain was coming out of its post-war austerity. White goods were becoming available and people were becoming a little more prosperous. Unfortunately, it hadn't quite reached the Mason's household. Even now Albert tells people, 'We had no fridge, no TV, no car, no phone and no central heating.'

Tall and well-built for his age Albert had a grown-up look when he was a child. Like a child who had gained several inches overnight. His trousers hung high on his ankles, and his thin sweaters baggy at the elbows. Arriving at school, he'd take off his jacket and roll his frayed sweater sleeves back to his elbows. He accompanied his mother to work every morning before school. She would wake him at 5 am and off they would go to a laundry business near to their home. In the winter months, the pavements would sometimes be wet with the night's rain, and made treacherous by the cold temperature, casting the rain to ice. His feet would freeze within minutes, because of the cardboard stuck in his shoes, to block the holes that had worn through. Once they arrived at Florence's work, he would help her fold and pack the laundry ready for distribution that day. When they'd finished, she would take him home to get ready for school, then leave to do her cleaning job at the local biscuit factory. At 3.30 pm she would make her way to her third job, cleaning at the local school where Albert and Jack were pupils.

Albert now hears people talking about their wonderful childhoods. But for him, it was deprivation and struggle. He tells friends and anyone else who would listen, 'I only had one pair of shoes, and they needed to last the whole year.'
In those days Albert was a street urchin and because of his size, he was the leader of the street gang that gathered in Bagleys Lane. He was never a lonely child, both his mother and father's parents lived in nearby William Parnell House, which is part of the Sands End area of Fulham and known as the 'tough' end of Fulham. Made up of terraced houses, Sands End became recognised as a close-knit working-class community. In the industrial heartland of Fulham. With its gas works, power station, biscuit factory and petrol depot. The area employed generations of local families. From the end of the Second World War the warehouses, works and wharves closed down. Leaving it a near wasteland by the 1980s.
The sixties began bleakly, but by the end of the decade, people were full of hope and optimism for a better future.

It was the time of change. If you shut your eyes for a second, you would have missed it. It was a period which allowed people, liberty and individuality and Albert knew he wanted a part, from an early age.

Albert met his wife, Jayne at the Hammersmith Palais in the summer of 1979, and married her three years later. They have one daughter, Olivia. Soon after they married, they found they wanted different things out of life and knew within months their marriage was a terrible mistake. After Jayne married Albert, friends and relatives noticed shifts in her personality. She lacked confidence and exhibited low self-esteem. Jayne told her closest friends she'd become like an extinguished fire and sensed she was plummeting over the edge into darkness. Most days she'd feel on edge, finding herself thinking negatively about herself, feeling hopeless and incompetent. Daily panic attacks stopped her going into shops because she couldn't stand other people being around her. Even getting to work became an ordeal. She felt so run-down she wasn't able to cope with even the basics.

Daily, she witnessed Albert's bouts of paranoia and experienced his false allegations, pathological jealousy and impulsive decision-making. It started with little things but progressed to more sinister accusations as the months went on. The more she tried to appease him, the more he accused her. He was seeing her car where her car had never been. He told her his friends were telling him about the things she was getting up to. She questioned her sanity and reality and felt she was in some twilight zone.

They are still married but live separate lives. Albert sometimes stays at their Chelsea Harbour property on rare occasions, when it served him. But most of the time he lives at his house in Holland Park, Notting Hill Gate.

Albert was seven when his father George committed suicide. When Albert returned home from school that day, Florence told him to sit down at the kitchen table and that she needed to explain something to him. Albert never forgot it and was never the same person again. His father George left school with no qualifications and joined the local laundry business as a van driver. After he married Florence, he studied in the evenings and passed accounting exams. He then left the laundry business, to provide a better life for Florence and the boys. Before his death, he worked for a bank in the City of London. When he started at the bank, some of his colleagues made it plain; they were not interested in working or socialising with him. George knew it was because he came from a working-class family and had the wrong accent. He resolved to keep his head down and focus on his work. Enthusiastic to learn, he took the bullying as banter. Not only would they not accept him, but they tried their best to crush him and succeeded. Florence knew George's anxiety going to work was making him sick with fear. So, booked an appointment for him to visit the doctor, who prescribed him antidepressants. Over the following months George's health broke down, and he lost over two stone. His treatment at work was subtle and cumulative. He would stay late in the office most evenings, working twelve-hour days. Taking on more and more work, he was determined to prove he was as good as they were. When he pointed out to his boss, he was working the extra hours. His boss sneered at him, stating he was staying late, to correct all the errors he had made during the day.

The night before he died, he'd been pacing around the house, saying, 'I have to quit, I can't go back there.' Again, and again. He had tried to end his life with an overdose, several months before but without success. Florence had ensured he took his medication, until the final month of his life, when she had fallen ill herself. In the last weeks of his life, the verbal abuse from his colleagues cut much deeper into him. After he died, Florence told the inquest in Hammersmith. He'd arrived at work a week after the overdose, and greeted by a colleague who declared, 'Oh, you're are alive then, don't worry we haven't missed you.'

Remarks such as, 'Have you taken your happy pills, George, you will need them today, became a regular occurrence. When George complained about the abuse, his boss, replied laughing, 'Those wicked boys, I'll have a word with them but never did. The final straw was when two work colleagues locked him in a stationery cupboard. They then set about burning his suit jacket, which hung on the back of his chair. That afternoon, Florence found him hanging when she returned from work. He had plummeted from the landing.

Albert's stomach still lurches with nausea whenever he sees the logo of the bank where his father had worked. Florence told people Albert was never the same person again after she told him. Florence took him to see a doctor, and the doctor referred to a psychiatrist. The psychiatrist told Florence, in time Albert's problems would resolve themselves. But they never did. As a child, he'd get into fights with other kids, some much older than him. Albert would also attack his mother, with uncontrolled rage. In his teenage years, he suffered from immaturity, temper tantrums and an inability to cope

with life. Albert cried in situations in which you would not expect, from someone of his age. He also experienced bouts of distorted thinking and mood swings.
Educated at St Henry's School, he left at fifteen and joined his uncle Tommy's trading business and soon moved up the ranks in the company. When Tommy retired in the mid-80s, Albert took over the business. He had big ideas and bought out smaller firms, in and around West London. His brutal business tactics included undercutting rivals and poaching their best staff. This gave him a reputation of a predator. He's exhibited similar tactics in all other ventures he's taken on throughout his life.
Albert Mason is now one of the most charismatic, captivating businessman in London. He has bold ideas, energy, immense charm, and a flair for personal publicity. With the unpolished diction of his West London upbringing, he's the appearance and the image of a man, who had fought his way to the top. After an early life of having nothing.

In the years of growing his business he's encountered plenty of snobbery and pretension in the corporate world he mixed in. He detested snobbery and thought the root of it was a lack of vision. From the outset, he decided he would advance and gain power. And would never tolerate snobbery or bullying, no matter what it took. Little did he know he would turn into the biggest bully and snob of them all.
Albert never had a conscience. No matter what he'd done or continued to do, he needed to be in control and have things his way, and would do whatever he needed to do to get it. Albert only loves himself and thinks he is the best at whatever he does even if he's rubbish at it.

Everyone's world revolves around his, and no one else matters. When his mother died, on the outside he showed sadness, but on the inside, he didn't feel a thing. Throughout his life and business career, he'd take credit for other people's work, by being their boss or having minimal input. He's a person who tries to dictate how everything's done and is obsessive with detail. To the point, if he were talking to someone, he would adjust their jacket, if he felt it was out of place. If he entered someone's office and their desk was untidy, to their astonishment he would tidy it for them.
He has an unrealistic sense of superiority. Never self-doubting in elite surroundings and is self-assured in the boardroom. He's achieved his vast wealth by breaking every rule in the book. Now at his peak, he's courted from every corner of the City of London.

His business career has never been without its problems. In the 1990 recession, a series of troubling property deals caused the company profits to dive. His company all but wiped out. But with his brutal, hard-nosed tactics, he came fighting back even stronger. His company Nasom Leisure is now worth over nine hundred million pounds on the stock market. With his fortune estimated at six hundred and fifty million pounds. The company's assets cover a spectrum of leisure businesses, including theatres, sports centres, hotels and various other developments spread across the United Kingdom. His companies employ over 1,000 people, according to City Business Magazine.

CHAPTER
10

1998

With butterflies in her stomach and her head buzzing, Julia's pacing up and down, as if determined to wear out the carpet. Rocking on her heels, she's waiting for Luca to pick her up for their first date. Glancing at her watch for the fifth time in ten minutes, she scans the street below. Standing at the mirror waiting for a knock on the door, she can't stand still, her body jiggling and dancing as she tidies her makeup.

Two years have passed since a terrible car crash killed her parents. But even now when she looks in the mirror, she sees hurt and unhappiness in her face. Luca came into Julia's life like a flashbulb, all at once, brightly and instantaneously. She knows her mum would have been so excited for her tonight and would have stayed up for her, to see how her date with Luca had gone.

Seeing Luca exiting his car and walking towards the front door, she thinks to herself, 'I feel like eating him up. His voice is so warm and rich, and there's something so sexy in that vulnerable boyish look of his.'

Hearing a gentle knock on the door, Luca greets her, giving her a soft kiss on the cheek. They descend the steps arm in arm, into the warm summer evening air. Hailing a cab in Wandsworth Bridge Road, they head to the Golden Gloves pub, in Fulham Palace Road. It was to be a night that would transform their lives forever.

It's still early evening when they arrive, and the pub is quiet. They order their meals and Luca gets some drinks. The evening didn't get off to the best of starts.

Everything was going well until the waitress brought the main courses to the table. Julia's drizzling lemon on her fish and squirts Luca straight in the eye. Luca looks at her with his good eye, let's out a short laugh and shakes his head. People standing at the bar turn. As they both fall about in fits of laughter, that echo around the pub. Resuming their meals, Luca looks over at her. Her face is serene yet full of strength and character. At that moment, he wants to immerse her in his arms and never let her go. But first things first, he had to get through tonight.

At first, Julia thinks he's shy, but as the night goes on, she senses him growing in confidence. There's something she instinctively likes about him, but can't explain it. Since the unfortunate deaths of her parents, Julia's proficient at concealing her broken insides. She'd always believed trust must come before love. But that night, she understood, love and trust could appear at the same time. Something felt right about Luca Rossi.

Towards the end of the evening, Julia feels Luca move closer. spotting something in her hair.
Gathering her hair at the side he slides it down her hair strands. She didn't know what it was, a small leaf or something of that nature. But at that moment, she felt special; it was a sensitive act.
   Most other guys would have grunted, 'You've got something in your hair'.
   With Luca it was different, he had an attentive side she hadn't experienced before with boys she had dated. Leaving the pub at 10.30 pm it's still warm, so they walk back part of the way to Julia's flat. Strolling arm in arm along Fulham Palace Road. The sky is dark and clear

and ribbons of silver moonlight are streaking through the gaps in the trees, creating shadows around them. Reaching Lillie Road, Luca hails a cab and asks the driver to take them to the junction of Wandsworth Bridge Road and Hazlebury Road.

Exiting the cab at the top of Julia's road; the air is sweet and the breeze refreshing. A white string of stars is littering the sky above them, as they stand at the foot of the steps that lead to Julia's front door. Staring at each other for what seems an age, Julia drops her gaze. Looking up at him, a subtle glow of pink blushes her cheeks, which makes her look defenceless. Wrapping his arms around her shoulders, he draws her close, caressing her arms. Holding his breath, she leans up onto the tips of her toes and presses her soft sweet lips to his. Luca pulls her towards him, his powerful muscular arms encircling her waist. Freeing one of his hands he traces his index finger along the line of her delicate jaw. With both hands framing her face, his lips ravish hers. Goosebumps pucker her skin, her heart somersaulting in her chest. He's so tender and caring; he steals her heart there and then.

Two years later Luca proposed to Julia on a short Christmas shopping trip in Paris. They'd come out of a restaurant, the snow falling hard. Luca pulled Julia close and whispered, 'I love you more than anything in this entire world.'

Welling up, he then told her, 'I want to be with you for the rest of my life.'

Before she knew it, he reached into his pocket, went down on one knee and asked her to marry him. With tears in her eyes she told him, she loved him more than words could express. Beaming at him with a saucy grin she asked, 'When?'

When Julia walked out on Luca twelve months ago, he was distraught. He remembers Julia looking at him as a stranger. Her words falling from her mouth and landing in his guts, feeling like someone had shot him. He had thought their marriage unbreakable and had taken their marriage for granted.

Through text messages, Luca had agreed to meet Julia, at Dino's restaurant, inside the Fulham Broadway Station shopping complex. She wanted to discuss the children and arrange for him to see them regularly. Arriving at Dino's before Julia he sits by the window, overlooking the old Town Hall. Having not seen her for three months he's feeling apprehensive. Ordering a double espresso, he waits, gazing out of the window onto the bustling Fulham Road. A few minutes later he spots Julia crossing the road and notices her walk is uncertain, as though her steps are out of sync. Dressed in a plain knee-length French navy blue dress, which is hugging her extraordinary figure, she strolls into the restaurant, looking around for Luca. Not disguising her emotions well, her pain is evident. Finding him sitting by the window, she approaches. Luca stands and gives her an awkward peck on the cheek and she sits down opposite him. Noticing she's still wearing her wedding and engagement rings. It makes his heart beat faster and somehow makes him feel content.

With the sun streaming in through the window, a waitress appears, and Julia orders a skinny latte. At first, there's a lack of eye contact. Their knees touch under the table. Removing her elbows from the table she sits back. Pulling her legs nearer to her as though being defensive.

Luca breaking the silence, asks a terrible cliché of a question, 'How have you been keeping?

Emotionless, she snaps back, 'Fine thanks.'

Staying silent, she stares at him, her wide blue eyes becoming glossy and wet. Turning away, trying to hide the sadness in his eyes, he refuses to let his tears flow. Looking back at her he sees her bottom lip quivering as she tries to speak. There's a thickness in her throat and the words do not appear.

She stands to leave. Luca smiles at her and pleads, 'Please stay and talk.'

Sitting back down she takes a sip of her coffee. Luca's expression changes, his smile fades, his face taking on an enquiring intensity. Detecting there's something wrong, he asks, 'Is everything ok? You appeared to be limping when you came in.'

Appearing to lighten up she answers, 'No I'm fine, a sprained ankle that's all.'

He could tell she was lying.
Chatting for over an hour, it's as though they'd never parted. Talking about the children and how they were getting on at school.

Luca looking into her in the eyes tells her, 'I miss you and the girls so much.'

Her reply is not what he wanted, 'I need to go now. I need to pick the girls up.'

'I can't take this anymore, Julia.'

With tears in his eyes he tells her, 'When you left that Sunday afternoon, you broke my heart. The biggest mistake I made was thinking, my career mattered. I missed so many precious years with you and the girls. I spent many of those hours in a dark office, or on some all-night stakeout in a smelly cramped van. Now I'm nothing but a shell and bereft of a love, I took for granted. My heart's broken Julia, and I can't stop loving you.'

His words shake her lean frame, and she's sent tumbling over the edge into uncontrollable sobs, which threaten to split her apart.

She whispers, 'You told me I should leave you. To go far away and never come back. I did and gave up on the only person I have ever loved. You took root in me in a way no one else as ever done.' She shakes her head, 'I am sorry Luca, I can't do it again.'

He puts out his hands and holds hers across the table, trying to calm her. It crosses his mind again. There's got to be something else; she was not telling him.

Getting to her feet, she tells him, 'I must go now, I'll be late for the girls.'

Luca asks, 'Could we meet again, soon?'

Sitting back down, wiping her eyes, she asks him, 'Why don't you come over to my place for lunch on Sunday and see the girls?'

Kissing him on the cheek, she leaves. He watches as she passes the window and crosses the Fulham Road. She's dawdling, almost mechanical. It's like her brain's struggling to tell her feet to take the next step. With shoulders slumped, eyes cast down in a sad stare, his heart sears with pain. He knows he needs to get back to work, but it all seems so meaningless now.

CHAPTER
11

Sam had arranged to meet Rick for a coffee, at Gina's Café in Limerston Street, Chelsea, before a team briefing at 8.30 am. Pacing along the Kings Road towards the World's End. Fumes from the perpetual morning traffic are invading her lungs, making her eye's water, turning into Limerston Street. She finds the tiny café nestling amongst large houses on either side like it's hiding in the shade from the early morning sunlight. She's about to enter when she hears a baby screaming, its mother ignoring it, while she barks into her mobile phone, crossing the road.

Entering the café, standing in front of her in the queue, is a gorgeous young blond girl. Dressed in a tight white t-shirt and pale blue Levi jeans, in Sam's eyes, she looked perfect. Detecting the essence of an exquisite fragrance lingering in the air, Sam closes her eyes, and the aroma floods her brain with endorphins. Glancing down, she checks the girl's hand for a wedding ring, none. Smiling to herself, she considers how to start a conversation. Bumping into her, fainting, or dropping something on her foot? Sam's daydreaming stops when a tanned dark headed man enters and throws his arms around the girl. As they exchange doe-eyed looks of love, Sam thinks, 'Damn, not gay then.'

Paying for her latte she sits down, two tables along from a group of loud builders, who are eating their breakfasts as if it was their last meal. One builder, who has most of his teeth missing, leers at her. Rolling her eyes at him, she looks the other way.

Sam is thirty-four, attractive and stands at five-foot-six. She is lissom and could easily pass for twenty. She has jet black hair, cut into a bob, high cheekbones and bright green sparkling eyes. Her colleagues and friends call her the human blur. After even a short time with Sam, your head would spin like a helicopter blade out of control. Her minds always filled with questions and opinions about everything. And if people didn't agree with her, she wasn't angry. She would sympathise with them for not understanding it her way.

In her life, she'd met women who were adamant, they were not attracted to other women in their teenage years but awakened later in life. But Sam knew she was gay from an early age. In her fourth year at Hurlingham Girls School, she remembers one day looking at her best friend at the time Kate, realising she had feelings for her. Sam's affections and emotions were different and too strong for just a friendship. She had a crush on Kate and couldn't talk to her as a friend would do. It wasn't long before she realised; she wanted Kate sexually. Knowing she cared for Kate in a way that Kate could never reciprocate, she suppressed the crush and her feelings.

At 18, she finally acknowledged she was gay and started to feel good about herself. Becoming her true self, she quit fretting about what everybody else thought.

She now tells friends; coming out never ends. Saying, 'I'm always outing myself. For most people, heterosexuality is the default norm. Unless you are holding hands with your girlfriend.'

Arriving at 7.10 am, looking blurry-eyed, Rick calls over to Sam, 'Do you want another coffee?'

'No thanks, I'm fine.'

After getting his coffee, and ordering his food, he sits down opposite.

Sam teases, 'You look like a bloody Zombie.'

'Yes, I know Sam, I have a sleep disorder, it's called having children.'

A frown creases Sam's forehead, 'Any more news on the murdered girl?'

'Only that there was no DNA left at the scene and no CCTV. He knew what he was doing.'

Sam tells him, 'I keep finding myself thinking of the crime scene, and what that poor girl must have gone through. I am glad her father didn't get to see her in that state. Do you think there will be more?'

'We're dealing with a crazy bastard here Sam, being honest, yes I do.'

Shoving half the bacon sandwich into his mouth, he chews as though he'd not eaten for a week.

Sam tells him, 'People think of psychopaths as killers and outside society. But you could have one for a co-worker or a friend or even a partner. They lack empathy and scarcely feel emotion. Did you know? Ted Bundy, the American serial killer, told the authorities after his arrest, 'I'm the most cold-blooded son of a bitch you'll ever meet? I like to kill.'

Rick raises his eyebrows and chuckles, 'What are you trying to say, Sam?'

With traces of bread caught on his upper lip, and tomato sauce dripping onto the table, he demolishes the rest of his bacon sandwich.

Sam smiles at him and they get up to leave, for their meeting with Luca and the rest of the team.

CHAPTER
12

After her lunchtime shift, Martina is leaving the restaurant to meet a friend for a drink in Putney. Spotting Reg on the other side of Harrington Road, she calls out to him, 'Where you off to Reg?'

'On my way home, I've just finished my shift at the museum.'

'Would you like a lift? I'm going your way?'

'Only if you don't mind.'

Reg gets into Martina's silver Range Rover and they drive off towards Fulham. Looking over at Reg, his cheeks are so hollow Martina can virtually see through them. A few hundred yards along the road Martina slyly opens her window. A putrid aroma seems to follow Reg everywhere he goes. Grinning, she remembers Marie telling her in mangled English, 'He stinks like a llama's bum.'

She now wishes she hadn't offered him a lift. Reg never said much, but when he did, it was short and to the point. He's a strange-looking man and gives most people he meets the creeps.

Trying to break the silence, she asks, 'What are you up to this afternoon Reg?'

'Not much.' He says no more until Martina turns the corner, into Peterborough Road, 'What number Reg?'

'42, please.'

Parking up opposite the house, 'Here you go Reg, is it the one next door to the derelict one?'

'No, that's number 42, where I live.'

Embarrassed, she thinks the grim, miserable building is the worst excuse for a house she'd ever encountered, it looks more like an abandoned mental asylum, than a once charming home.

'Do you live alone Reg?'

'No, I have mum living with me, but she's no trouble.'

Bewildered, she was sure Maria had told her his mother died, many years ago. Getting out of the car, he waves back at Martina, as he wanders across the road towards the dilapidated house. Driving off, she opens all four windows of the Range Rover. With the afternoon sunlight warming its grey brick walls, the years have accomplished irreversible deeds upon the once proud property. The house is a crumbled beauty of an era long past. The wooden frames of the windows are rotting, and flakes of yellowing paint lay like dandruff on its windowsills. Next to the refurbished houses in the street, the house looks like it had been beamed in from an old horror movie, and was refusing to die. Removing his key from his belt, Reg lets himself into the house, which has a feeling of comfortable decay.

Reg calls up the stairs, 'Mum. It's only me. Are you ok?' The exposed wooden floorboards creak and groan beneath his feet as if the house is in its death throws. The stink of damp wafts through the air. Dust lies on every surface like dirty snow and sections of the ceiling hang limp in the air. The contents of the house are a time-warp of long-forgotten brands. Sepia photographs adorn the walls; it's like a living museum. It looks like no one had purchased anything new since the 50s. Entering the kitchen, he opens the dirty curtains, and glimmers of the late afternoon sun beam through the decaying windows. His presence makes the resident spiders scurry into dark corners. Their webs flapping in silence, clasping to the walls like ghostlike fingers.

Looking up at the ceiling he hollers, 'Do you want a cup of tea mum? You've been quiet since I came in. Martina from the restaurant gave me a lift home. She's a kind woman; she always chats with me when I'm working at the restaurant. I was working at the V&A this morning; I got in nice and early. Before I started on my chores, I had two hours exploring more of the boarded-up tunnels and passages in the basement. There was muck and dust everywhere; I don't think anyone had been down there for years. I would have asked Martina in for a cup of tea, but I thought you might not be up to it. Have you heard anything from them bastards next door today?'

He thinks to himself, 'One day I'll walk straight in there and smash the lot of them with my lump hammer. No one will care. They make mum's life a misery, and one day they will pay for it.'

CHAPTER 13

Waking early Sunday morning Luca has an extraordinary sense of optimism. An emotion he hasn't had in months. He's visiting Julia and the girls for lunch. He showers, dresses and turns off his mobile; no one is going distract him today. Including calls from work. Leaving the house at 1.30 pm, he decides to walk to Julia's flat, which is on the other side of Fulham. Making his way down Parsons Green Lane, he turns left onto Fulham Road. The afternoon sun has brought the streets alive. A great river of people, red buses and black cabs are slivering amongst the buildings. He's never liked the transformation and gentrification that's changed this part of London. Forty years ago, Fulham was a working-class area, full of rented houses and a few dodgy estates. It's now filled with shops, bars, boutiques and restaurants — city bonuses producing a massive hike in house prices. Fulham is now part of London's banker belt, which spreads in a crescent through South West London. Starting in Chelsea and sweeping through Fulham before it crosses the Thames and curves round to Putney, Barnes, Wandsworth and Clapham. Properties in Fulham can now sell for fortunes. To Luca, it seems a million miles away from his childhood home in William Parnell House.

Julia woke that morning with a revived enthusiasm. She'd been up since 6.30 am, sprucing up the flat and preparing Sunday lunch. So lost in creating scenarios for the day; her brain feeling like it's full of static. With a cool morning breeze flowing in through the kitchen window, and the girls still tucked up in their beds. She's has plenty of time to think about the day ahead. Struggling to get out of bed most days, she's now finding plenty of ways to cope. To Julia the fatigue appears as though she's being weighted down. As if she is trying to walk through a deep muddy bog, carrying bags full of rocks. Most days her brain goes foggy and she can't think. She tells her friends the hardest part of the fatigue is waking up from a night of sleep, but then too tired to get out of bed. It frustrates her to be so tired after resting and deflating her, before her day even starts. Julia's only fallen in love once in her life, and Luca never leaves her mind; he's in her thoughts day and night. She loses those thoughts when Amalee stumbles into the room. With her eyes full of joy, she asks, 'When will daddy be here, mummy?'

Julia laughs, telling her, 'Amalee, it's only seven o'clock. He won't be here until two o'clock.'

Amalee moves like an octopus, limbs moving according to the chaos theory, rather than anything a social scientist could explain. Her eyes are ablaze; every muscle needs to run, dance and jump. Thirty seconds later Darcy enters the kitchen, wondering what all the commotion's about.

Rubbing her eye's, she asks, 'Can I have my breakfast please mummy?'

Until Luca's promotion to DI three years ago, all was well with their marriage, but things soon changed. Julia found herself on her own with the girls for long periods of time. Luca left her to do it all. The crying, laughing, cooking, cleaning and cuddling them into bed.
Glancing at her phone for the third time in ten minutes, the morning is now ebbing slower than an asthmatic snail. As the morning goes on she thinks, is she strong

enough to risk going through it all over again? She ignores the thoughts and sets about preparing Luca's favourite, roast beef and Yorkshire pudding.

Luca arrives at Julia's flat, on the ground floor of an impressive red-bricked mansion block, at 2 pm. The block stands opposite terraced houses which over the last two decades have doubled in size, with an array of Tardis-like loft and basement extensions. As a result, the road has seen a rise in the number of affluent professionals, employed in the banking and hedge fund industries living there.

Taking a deep breath, he paces towards the entrance. His anxiety intensifying as he gets closer to the door. Holding a bunch of red roses in his hand, he presses the doorbell and waits. Hearing the scampering and shrieking of Amalee and Darcy, making their way to the door, like of a herd of stampeding wildebeest. As the door opens the girls hug and kiss him as though they'd not seen him in months. Entering the hall, the smell of the roast dinner hits him.

Coming out of the kitchen looking ravishing, a sparkling smile breaking across Julia's beautiful face. Approaching she gives him a peck on the cheek and steers him into the lounge.

Before he can sit down, Amalee asks, 'Daddy can we go to the park after lunch?'

Glancing over at Luca, Julia tells Amalee, 'Of course we can.'

Staring at Julia, Luca tells Amalee, 'Mummy might come as well?'

Julia smiles, 'We can take a walk to Bishops Park if you like?'

Darcy interrupts, 'Can I tell you a joke Daddy?'

'Yes, I would love to hear it. It's not rude, is it?'

Giggling she tells him, 'No it isn't daddy. Did you hear about the crook who stole a calendar?'

Shaking his head, 'No, I haven't.'

Darcy breaks into fits of laughter, 'He got twelve months.'

Luca throws back his head, roaring with laughter, 'That's brilliant, I will tell everyone at the station tomorrow.'

At first, it's a strange atmosphere for Luca, he feels like a guest in his own home, but he's happy for the first time in months. The room is elegant in a minimalist way. There's a lack of luxury but no shortage of ambience. Sitting back relaxing, he feels a bubble of joy rising inside him. Sitting in the lounge after lunch with the girls, jumping all over him, Julia enters. With her head held high and a grin on her red lips, she beams, 'Shall we go to the park, then?'

The sky is a cloudless blue as they stroll through the back streets towards Bishops Park. They arrive at the park fifteen minutes later. The park is in the full thrust of summer. Luca can hear children shrieking with joy and dogs barking in the distance. The trees are a riot of colour, and leaves are pirouetting through the air above them. For Luca, it's odd being here again after so long. But despite the time he'd been away, he still remembers everything about the place. Somehow, he'd forgotten his discomfort and heartache and is in no rush to go home soon. The summer sun is gentle as Darcy and Amalee chase each other across the grass field.
Plenty of other families with the same idea are taking advantage of the cool breeze coming off the river.

Luca's talking to Amalee, when he catches Darcy, who is walking in front with Julia, asking her, 'Mummy are you going to the hospital again tomorrow?'

Julia replies, whispering, 'No not this week my love.'

'I don't like you going to the hospital Mummy.'

Luca, says nothing, grabbing Amalee, tickling her under her arms. She screams and giggles, 'Don't Daddy, I'll wet myself.' At that moment, she sounded just like Julia, all those years ago the night they met. Luca buys ice creams and they sit on the grass. Julia inhales the fresh air around her and smiles her first natural smile in months. It's a wonderful sight, Darcy's pulling up handfuls of grass, letting it blow away in the breeze. Amalee is chasing all over the field trying to catch it. Finishing their ice creams, they stroll along the riverside to Putney Bridge. With the sun sparkling in the infinite blue sky, the Thames is flowing like an endless liquefied mirror into the distance. It's gentle, seductive curves, calm and innocuous.

With the girls walking on ahead, Luca tells Julia, 'You are so lucky to have this on your doorstep. I have great memories of this place. I remember coming here with my mates when I was a kid, to play football whenever I could. I remember we chased each other, in and out of the bushes along the Stevenage Road side of the park, trying to avoid the park keepers.'

Luca reminisces, 'Mum brought us here in the school summer holidays for picnics.' He laughs, 'She always seemed to pack Heinz Sandwich Spread filled rolls. And if we were good, she would take us to Santilli's ice-cream van over by the green exit gate.

He adds 'I remember spending many lively hours in the small lake adjacent to the sand pit; we loved trying to swim in the deep end. It was only two feet deep. Do you bring the girls here a lot?'

A cheerful Julia replies 'Yes, they love it over here. Would you believe the locals now call the sandpit and paddling pool, an urban beach?'

Luca laughs out loud, 'No, you are joking?'

She tells him, 'We go to the pond to feed the birds. It's beautiful; it's like being in the country, not in the middle of London.'

Leaning forward, he lowers his voice, 'I miss you and the girls so much. Do you get lonely?'

Julia's lips part in surprise, 'Yes, I do, all the time. What about you, has there been anybody else since we split?'

'No, never, I swear.'

A tremor touches her smooth sumptuous red lips, deep down she's delighted.

CHAPTER
14

A blow on the head wakes Eve Thomas. Opening her eyes to blackness, she realises her hands, feet and mouth are bound. Feeling drowsy, she asks herself where the hell she is? The only thing she remembers, is standing in a room with lots of people around her, laughing.
Tuning into the sound of an engine, she understands, she's in the boot of a car. Another bump jolts her upwards, this time she keeps her head down. She can smell the newness of the car, mixed with her fear. When her head clears, it still makes little sense. Panic hits her, and she screams, but little comes out because of the plastic tape covering her mouth. Kicking upwards at the boot lid, it doesn't budge; it only causes more pain in her cramp-ridden legs.
Like an explosion in her brain, she recalls a tall man wearing rubber gloves, placing one hand on her neck, and holding a syringe in the other. Danger shrieks through her head, and she prays.

   The car comes to a stop, and the engine dies. The only thing she can hear are her own stifled sobs. The boot springs open. Looking up squinting, a towering figure is scowling down at her. Through slits in his balaclava, his vicious eyes stare at her, with such a ferocity she shivers. Terrified and unable to move, she's helpless, as he stoops down and lifts her out of the boot of the car. Her nose fills with the musty odour of the sack he's now putting over her head.
Carrying her into the house, he sits her down on the cold

tiled floor. Gasping for air, she struggles trying to squirm across the room. Grabbing hold of her, he slams her against a wall. The only sounds she can hear now are footsteps, and the sound of her pulse throbbing in her ears. Feeling his fingers dig into her cheek, he pulls off the hood. Looking up at him, in the pale twilight of the room, she's terrified to the core. A deadly smear of amusement plays across his dark eyes. After he unties her, she pulls up her knees to her chest and wraps her arms around her shins and shuts her eyes. She'd experienced fear before, but nothing like this. Feeling his hand on her arm, her eyes snap open, taking away every feeling of safety she'd ever had.

Trying to move, she can't. She can see and hear what's going on, but her brain won't let her body cooperate. Touching the rim of her cold blue lips with the tip of his butcher's knife, he smirks, 'I'm going to cut you into little pieces.'

Before she can scream, the finely honed blade rips through her throat. Setting about her, he doesn't stop until there's any life's left in her young body.

CHAPTER 15

Arriving for work at 6 am, Martina enters the restaurant to the aroma of toasted bread and coffee. Franco's busy arranging pastries and other delicacies behind the glass display, which fronts the counter. Spotting her, he wipes his hands on his blue striped apron and blows her a kiss, 'Hi sis, how are you on this glorious morning?'

'I'm fine; you're cheerful this morning?'

'I'm always cheerful sis. Reg is in the kitchen, he was asking for you a few minutes ago.'

'What did he want?'

Franco quips, 'Something about taking you out tonight?'

Martina shakes her head, giving him gave him a wry look. Poking her tongue out at him she heads to the kitchen. She's about to push the door open when Reg, on the other side beats her to it.

'Hi Reg, were you looking for me?'

Flustered, he answers, 'Yes, I wanted to thank you for giving me a lift home, that's all.'

'No problem. Was your mum ok when you got in?'

Ignoring her comment, he scuttles back to the kitchen and down to the cellar. After the door closes, all she can smell is a waft of oil and piss, which seems to follow Reg everywhere.

Thirty minutes later, Reg comes out of the kitchen and tells Franco he'd finished in the cellar. After he leaves the restaurant for his shift at the V&A. A few seconds later Martina appears in the central part of the restaurant and whispers, 'Franco, has he gone?'

'Who Reg?'

'No, the bloody Dalai Lama. Why are we using that

man in our restaurant? He stinks the place out; do we need him?'

'He's ok sis, and he's cheap.'

'Well, he gives me the creeps.'

Franco brings over two cappuccinos, and they sit down at a table. Looking out on to Harrington Road, Franco asks, 'Have you heard from Luca?'

'No, but Julia phoned me last night and told me their Sunday lunch together went well. They visited Bishops Park in the afternoon with the girls.'

'That's great news sis, are you hopeful?'

She nods and takes a sip of her coffee, 'I think Julia's mind is clear and resolute. She told me it's as if the distance between them has narrowed. I didn't tell you, but a couple of weeks ago, she told me she'd been drinking heavy most nights after the girls had gone to bed?'

Franco responds, shaking his head, 'That's sad, but I'm sure they will be ok in the end. They love each other too much to part for good.'

'I hope so Franco.'

'Anyway sis, how's lover boy, Mason? I think Reg is getting jealous.'

She beams, 'I'm seeing him again on Wednesday evening.'

'Where's he taking you, somewhere posh and swanky?'

'If you must know, The Dorchester.'

'Are you sure about him, sis, he's got history you know.'

Martina frowns and asks, 'Have you been talking to Luca about him?'

He laughs, 'Of course I have, that's what brothers do. We've always looked out for you, you know that.'

'Well Franco, I'm a big girl now, so please leave it.'

Martina's shocked when Franco tells her, 'You probably

won't remember, but he lived near to us, when we lived in William Parnell House with mum and dad.'

'You are joking?'

'I'm not; he was trouble then, a real bully.'

Martina's a confident, beautiful woman who radiated classic Mediterranean beauty. Her dark Italian eyes are mesmeric. When her eyes meet someone else's, that someone usually smiled back. She has olive skin, sumptuous full lips, and hair that flows down her back like black ink. At forty-seven she's never married. She's had serious relationships in the past, but tells everyone; she's still looking for Mr Right. It's a running joke at the restaurant.

She met her last partner Paul, at a new year's party at a friend's house. Their relationship lasted for over two years. The physical part was good, but Paul never really showed her his heart. Weeks before their breakup, she thought he was looking at her like a stranger and she knew something was wrong. One morning she woke up, rolled over, reached for him, but he wasn't there. And never would be again. She was heartbroken for months; he'd drawn her in with a sweetness she'd never found before. He then betrayed her affections and left her heart in a shattered disarray of pieces. She thought she'd found the love of her life, but he didn't.

CHAPTER 16

Luca's about to leave the house when there's a knock on the door. Opening it, he's surprised when he sees Rick and all his bulk standing in the doorway, his massive arms folded.

Smiling he asks, 'Is your phone off, boss?'

'Sorry Rick, I was just going to call you, what's the matter?'

'We've got another murder.'

'Where?'

'Queensmill Road. An estate agent phoned it in an hour ago. Sam and uniform are attending.'

'Are there any other details?'

'Nothing yet.'

Driving to the scene, he asks, 'How did it go with Julia and the girls yesterday?'

'It went well to be honest, a lot better than I thought it was going to. Julia's flat is near to where we're heading now.'

'Seeing her again soon?'

'I hope so Rick; I'm missing the three of them so much.'

'Anyway, how's your daughter's relationship going?'

'It's not. She finished with him weeks ago, thank God. She brought another one home on Sunday, to introduce him. I don't know where she gets them from. Ugly wasn't the word. He had a face like a camel eating a lemon.'

Rick's comment brings a welcome smile to Luca's face.

The Merc tears along Fulham Palace Road with its sirens screaming. Turning left into Queensmill Road they arrive at the scene at 9.10 am. Luca can't see a taped cordon in place but spots three police cars parked up at different angles, opposite a school at the bottom of the road. A small crowd of neighbours are standing outside in the bright sunshine, trying to get a look at what's going on.

In the morning sunshine, Luca sees four young boys in Chelsea and Fulham shirts, kicking a football against a red-bricked graffiti-covered wall.

Luca tells Rick, 'I remember playing football against this school as a kid. They were good; we got hammered every time we played them.'

Rick raises his eyebrows, 'Let's hope the victim hasn't?'

Approaching the house along a short path. A previous owner had planted a rose garden, and although once cared for, it's now a wilderness, riddled with weeds and long brown grass.

Sam appears in the doorway in white overalls. Shielding her eyes from the sun she tells Luca, 'The scene is secure, the forensic team and doctor are on their way.'

She adds, 'Looks like the same MO boss. Her throat, lips, tongue and eyelids removed, and her head caved in.' Rick looks over at Luca and raises his eyebrows.

Putting on white protective overalls, Luca and Rick enter the Victorian terraced house. The renovated home is empty, without furnishings of any kind.

Sam points along the hall, 'She's in the kitchen, at the back.'

With no signs of blood in the hall, Luca stops at the kitchen door. Pushing his neck forward peering into the kitchen, an eerie silence bleeds into the room and generates an aura of coldness around him. His mouth slackens and his eyes widen, the scene looks like the gateway to hell; it's an abysmal sight.

The victim is sitting naked, looking like a ghoulish mannequin. Sitting on a rusty old garden chair, with her wrists tied behind her back. Her killer has bound her ankles to the front legs of the chair with rusty wire, which has cut into her flesh. The sickening smell of blood is blanketing the air. It appears as a special effects horror film crew had been working overtime. Droplets of blood have sprayed onto the newly decorated cornflower blue walls, making random patterns of scarlet. Her body has leaked pints of blood, creating a jagged red river across the white-tiled floor. Putting up his hand, he clears his throat, 'Let's wait for forensics and the doctor to get here.'

Standing in the hall he tells Rick, 'Some say when you're going to die, you'll know it. You will sense it when you wake up in the morning. You'll go through the day looking over your shoulder, seeing things that aren't there, hearing voices. And when your last minutes on this earth are ending, your life will flash before your eyes. You'll see your childhood, your wedding day, your children, and all these will pass before you instantaneously. I bet this poor girl never dreamed in a million years it would end like this.'

Leaving the murder scene Luca and Rick head for the car, Rick tells him, 'You were right he's struck again, what the fucking hell drives these psycho's?'

Luca muses, 'I don't think the killings are random. I think they are about power or revenge, or both. Think about it, removing the tongue, eyelids, mouth, smashing the brain. It's like the killer wants to take away any power the victims have.'

Rick tells Luca, 'I've seen a lot of things in this job, but these murders are brutal, beyond belief. What the hell do they get out of it?'

Luca responds 'Psychopaths see themselves as the centre of the universe. They get great enjoyment from torture and the slow death of their victims. It includes lust, thrill, gain and power. Many theorists point to the disturbed childhoods of serial killers, as a conceivable reason for their actions, but I am not convinced. They wish to play God and be in charge of life and death. And if they remain free, they will continue to commit their crimes. It gives them a huge rush of pleasure and an even deeper urge to kill.'

Sitting in the car, Luca calls the station and asks them to get everyone in for a briefing at 4 pm.

At the team briefing, Luca had told the team a local man had been released from prison recently, on parole. He'd maimed his victim by severing her lips and served nine years of a fifteen year sentence.

On their way to the man's address in Battersea, Rick tells Sam, 'This guy we're about to visit, was getting on a bit when he was convicted ten years ago. He's now in his mid-seventies; surely he can't be in the frame for the recent attacks?'

'I know what you mean; let's find out, we're here.'

Parking the car in Kyber Road, they exit and walk towards the suspect's grubby terraced house. With ninety-nine percent of the homes renovated, in the now popular road, the suspect's property sticks out a mile. The roof is sagging and parts of the guttering are swinging in the summer breeze. There's a gaping hole in the front window, covered by a piece of cardboard from a Kellogg's cornflake packet, and kept in place with strips of yellowing sellotape. Sam opens the creaking rusty cobwebbed laden gate, and they enter. The grass in the tiny front garden is full of weeds and dog shit.

Rick, who Sam once described as a cross between Rambo and Ray Winstone, hammers on the peeling dull brown door. Sam notices the curtains move on the house to their left. Rick, bangs on the door again, and a face appears at the window to the right of the door, then disappears.

Rick tells Sam, 'That was him at the window, he didn't look happy. He had a face like a dog licking piss off a stinging nettle.'

They hear someone call out, 'For fucks sake, hold on will you.'

The door opens, and the side of a man's face emerges. Rick holds up his ID in front of him and bellows 'Are you, Michael Lyons?'

'Who's asking?'

'I'm DS Rick James, and this is DS Sam Jones, could we have a word inside?'

Lyons sneers, his voice dry and precise, 'If you must.'

Standing in front of them is a frail decrepit-looking man with a week's growth of stubble, sporting a t-shirt from a band that had been in fashion in the early seventies. His eyes are small and has the face of a boxer who had lost all his fights. Leaning on the door frame for balance, the man pants for air. Holding the door open, Rick and Sam squeeze past, and an aroma of sweat, piss and alcohol hits them. Lyons has a fringe of grey-white hair around his bald, mottled scalp. With each movement he makes, there's a groan of old bones. Shuffling down the hallway, he shows them into the back room, where the last rays of the early evening sun are failing to get in. The net curtains that adorn the window are thick with dust. The place reeks of cigarettes and urine. Sam notices a bucket of piss standing in the corner of the filthy room. Looking over at Rick, Sam raises her eyebrow's in disbelief; the smell is off the charts. After several minutes of questioning, it's clear Michael Lyons can't possibly be the killer.

When they get outside Sam whispers, 'What a waste of time that was.'

Rick quips, 'Fucking hell, everyone has a right to be ugly, but he abuses the privilege.'

Crossing Battersea Bridge on the way back to the station, the sun is filling the sky with a deep red. Setting the clouds ablaze. 'Are you out tonight Sam?'

'A chance would be a fine thing.'

'Like that, is it?'

Sam, does not answer.

CHAPTER
17

After her conversation with Franco at the restaurant regarding Albert, Martina's been feeling anxious all day. She likes Albert but doesn't like the circles he moves in. To her, it all seems too contrived. She prefers to mix with down-to-earth people. Not the sycophantic counterfeits that follow Albert around town. Martina's always thought those types of people only respect people who have power. And are selective about who merits respect and who doesn't, based on what they personally got out of it.

Looking graceful in her form-fitting black dress, which flaunts and flatters in equal measure, she's putting on the finishing touches to her makeup in front of the mirror, when the intercom buzzes. Opening the door, she finds Albert standing in the doorway with a bunch of flowers, in all his grandeur — dressed in a black dinner suit and red bow tie. Showing a proud pleasant smile, he kisses her on both cheeks. In his sharp, penetrating voice, he tells her, 'You look as beautiful as ever.'

Descending the steps to the busy road, Albert opens the passenger door to his gleaming Bentley Continental and ushers her into the front seat. It's summer in the city; Gunter Grove is lined with trees, which are standing still in the warm balmy evening air. Turning right, onto Fulham Road, they head for the West End.

'What have you been up to today, Albert?'

'Just a few business meetings in the city, that's all, nothing special.'

He adds, 'You seem a bit uneasy tonight, are you ok?'

'I'm fine, just had a long day at the restaurant, that's

all. We were busy, all day.'

Pulling into the forecourt of The Dorchester Hotel, twenty minutes later. To Martina's astonishment the doorman immediately appears out of nowhere, and opens the passenger door, 'Good evening Madam, welcome to The Dorchester Hotel.'

Departing the Bentley, she spots Albert throwing his car keys to a porter, who gets into the car and drives it off to the underground car park. Arm in arm they stroll into the hotel.

When they enter, there's a mass of flawless glass everywhere. The room is flooded in a golden light, and an immense chandelier in the centre of the elaborate ceiling is making shadows, dance across the lavish room. The resident pianist is indulging in the splendour of 1930s glamour. Immaculately dressed and super attentive the staff are making Martina feel like royalty.
After pre-dinner cocktails, they're shown to their table in the spacious dining room.

Having just sat down, a woman appears at Albert's side. Wearing beautiful designer clothes, she talks with an upper-class accent that immediately grates on Martina's nerves.

Albert stands and introduces her, 'Martina this is my daughter Olivia.'

Olivia's skin is white as snow. Her lips are red as blood and has hair as black as coal. She reminds Martina of a wicked Snow Queen.

Smiling, Martina shakes her hand, 'Nice to meet you, Olivia.'

Ignoring Martina's greeting she looks Martina up and down, as though she's something dirty, someone has trod in. Olivia screws up her nose as if Martina smells like it too.

Martina thinks to herself, 'Stuck-up bitch. She probably spends her days following celebrities. The woman, nobody, knows spending her life learning about the lives of women, everyone knows, the stupid cow.'

Martina hated pretension and snobbery and had always thought a snob was anybody who takes a small part of you, and uses it to come to a firm conclusion. About how much of their attention we deserve. In the past that might have meant a snob being interested in your family and lineage. Nowadays, the snob cares about two things only; what you do for a living and who you know. And according to how you answer, snobs will either welcome us with broad smiles or swiftly abandon us.

Martina had thought tonight would be special, a chance to get to know the real Albert. But like previous dates with him, he's neglecting her shaking hands and embracing people all over the place. After dinner, they make their way to the bar. Martina consciously chooses a table with two chairs, and they sit down. She'd thought this would be an excellent chance to tie him down and chat. But within seconds, Albert is restless and is scanning the bar, to see if there is anybody he recognises.

Waving over to a portly man standing at the bar he tells Martina, 'See the man standing at the bar in the white jacket?

'Yes.'

He's a leading barrister, at Lincolns Inn Fields.'

'Albert, I'm not interested in him. I'm interested in you. Tell me about your family.'

Staring at her shocked, he enquires 'Why do you want to know about something like that?'

Dismayed at his response, before she can respond,

Albert stands up and saunters over to the man at the bar. They greet each other like long-lost brothers, all shaking hands and backslapping.

Martina's watching Albert and the man laughing and joking, when a woman appears at her side.

Extending her hand, the woman introduces herself, 'I'm the wife of Jonathan Bloom-Smyth.' Plonking herself down at the table, the woman looks over at Albert and the man, 'It looks like the boys are having a good chat at the bar.'

The woman is obese and draped in a super-sized emerald ball gown. Martina thinks to herself, 'If pigs could fly this woman would be the squadron leader.'

For the next twenty minutes, the woman bores Martina. In an unemotional boring drone, she tells Martina about her royal connections and her closeness to the Mayor of London. Martina can't wait for her to disappear. When Albert reappears, the arrogant woman retreats to the bar and her husband.

'Sorry Martina, were you having a good chat?'

'Are you joking?'

Albert's not amused and tells her, 'She's a well-connected lady?'

'I don't care how connected she is. If you want to know, she bored me shitless.'

Looking at her with distaste he slumps back in the chair and asks, 'What is bloody wrong with you tonight?'

'Oh, I'm fine, but I would like to talk to you at some point this evening.'

Shaking his head in annoyance, he asks, 'Let's have another drink.' Getting up, he strolls over to the bar. When he returns with their drinks, he's more attentive towards Martina.

Looking at her, he smiles, 'Why don't you come over to

my place and have dinner, later this week? We can talk much better there, just the two of us. What do you say?'

Martina raises her glass, 'That would be nice. I look forward to it.'

CHAPTER
18

The sky is electric blue and there's not a breeze in the air, when Julia drops Amalee and Darcy off at Munster Road School at 8.45 am. Kissing the girls, they say their goodbyes and Julia heads for the Chelsea and Westminster Hospital. For her appointment with her neurologist at 10 am.

Julia was born at her parent's terraced house in Dawes Road Fulham in 1973. She'd just celebrated her 18th birthday when she received the devastating news, both of her parents had been killed in a car crash while on holiday in Andalusia, Spain.

Her parents were returning to their villa when a lorry crossed into their path. The lorry driver had been on his mobile phone when he ran through a red light, setting off a chain reaction. Julia's parent's car swerved to avoid an oncoming vehicle - but failed. The oncoming vehicle hit them, flipping their car over. Their car continued skidding along the road on its roof, before hitting a tree and bursting into flames. When Medics arrived, they pronounced her father dead at the scene. The ambulance took Julia's mother to the hospital, with traumatic head injuries and burns. She died after two hours on the operating table.

When local Police told Julia of the news, pain seared through her body taking away every feeling of love and safety she'd ever had. Braking down, she dropped to her knees, feeling as though someone had pulled her last breath from her lungs. With her parents gone, Julia was alone, other than two elderly aunts who lived in Devon.

After her parents died, Julia told friends 'I'm

incomplete without them. They were everything — my heart, my blood, my breath, my motivation.'

From the day they died, she wasn't a girl anymore, and never would be again. In the weeks that followed she was more scared of living than dying. As the months passed, she felt isolated with no one to look out for her. Grief and depression threatened to kill her soul. She described to friends her grief was like looking through a one-way window. You could see others, but they couldn't see you. She found it hard to understand how the world could go on when her life had stopped.

A photograph was all it took for the tears to burst her dam of restraint. Her best memories were the cruellest, cutting her insides as if they were slivers of glass. She remembers as a little girl her dad would lift her upon his shoulders or flinging her around by her arms and legs in the backyard, while she screamed and laughed. Her dad had hands like shovels and eyes that twinkled. Julia loved it when he told her his funny jokes, and tall tales of his youth.

She was trying to figure out how to live her life again. When she met Luca, he changed her life. For days after their first date, he invaded her thoughts constantly. He became her rock, and she felt safe around him. Having stolen each other's heart's, they became inseparable.

Three months after she left Luca, she started having bouts of blurred vision, so she booked an appointment with her optician. The optician gave her the usual tests, but couldn't find any problems with her eyes. So, he advised her to make an appointment with her GP. At the appointment with the GP, she disclosed other symptoms, including tingling and numbness in her fingers and bouts of fatigue. The doctor referred her to the neurological department at the Chelsea and Westminster

Hospital. After various tests and MRI scans, the consultant diagnosed her with Multiple Sclerosis.

Certain moments in life seem frozen in time, like a photograph. When Julia received her MS diagnosis, it was one of those. She still pictures the dour clinical room, with its blank white walls and harsh bright lighting. She remembers the soulless blank features of the neurologist. Who with no emotion told her, 'The scans show lesions on your brain, Mrs Rossi. I am one hundred percent certain you have Multiple Sclerosis. Do you have any questions?'

The doctor's words came slowly, as from a great distance.

The doctor's cold diagnosis rendered her speechless. On the way out she clamped her lips shut, to imprison the sobs that threatened to burst free. She left the hospital desperate and alone. When she reached her flat, she faced the sad truth of the situation. Sitting in silence on the sofa, she lowered her head, tears filled her eyes and trekked down her face. Licking her salty tears away, feeling broken she couldn't call her parents to tell them the news. And she didn't want to burden her best friend Tina, who was going through a severe illness of her own. All she wanted was to be in the strong arms of her only love, Luca. It was at this point she realised she couldn't live without him. Even now the memories of his love, fill her every waking moment.

After the initial shock of the diagnosis, she experienced a range of powerful emotions. All she could think was her MS would lead to a quick progressive disability. Leading to paralysis, pain, blindness, a wheelchair and death by choking.

Over the last two months, she's also had trouble with her balance and more extended bouts of fatigue. The MS makes her feel like every muscle in her body is giving up.

She craves sleep, a warm bed and beautiful dreams. But the pain of the MS won't let her. She also struggles most days psychologically. To escape the concern and worry, she lives by the mantra; it could always be worse. There's still something to be grateful for, no matter how small. Fear of the future is now her most significant worry because of the girls.

CHAPTER
19

Pulling his car to a stop outside the Cumberland Arms. Albert sits for a few seconds listening to the end of a Frank Sinatra track. Entering the pub at 10 pm for his meeting with Tony Daniels, he has a severe look on his face. If Albert had known failure in his life, it never showed. Stomping across the floor like he owned the place, he scans the bar that's crammed with punters. Looking up from their beers they don't recognise him, so their heads drop, to focus back on their drinks. Squinting to let in sufficient light, Albert navigates his way to Tony Daniels, who's sitting on his own on the far side of the pub, strumming his fingers on the table with one hand and holding a pint of lager in the other.

Tony Daniels, otherwise known as 'Mad Maltese Tony' is a long-time associate of Albert. He's a well-known gangster involved in extortion and drug trafficking in South and West London. His trademark is to carve M for mad on his victim's face, with a knife. Despite being connected to at least two murders, Fulham born Daniels has escaped justice on both counts. Recently Tony and his brother Danny have got involved in, importing guns from Eastern Europe. This has coincided with a rise in shootings in drugs turf wars in South London. Albert has used Daniels and his gang for ten years, to sort out disputes with business rivals. Or anyone else he needed sorting.

Tony and his brother Danny's talent to escape justice has given them an air of indestructibility. Fuelling the belief, they have police officers on their payroll. Even jurors are not immune from their menaces. The brothers began their criminal careers in their teens. Extorting money from local shops and market traders, close to their home in Bagleys Lane.

Albert's not happy; they are meeting today to discuss a series of tit-for-tat clashes between Tony and another gang, the Johnson's, who protected a business rival of Albert's. It began two months ago with an altercation in a snooker hall in Hammersmith Broadway. After the initial spat, tensions heightened, finally erupting when one of Tony's closest friends Jimmy Galvin had a baseball bat smashed over his skull several times, outside the Greyhound pub in Fulham Palace Road. And is still in intensive care.

Freddie and Vic Johnson are violent thugs, who stop at nothing. Tony couldn't let them get away with it and felt he needed to be decisive and retaliate. Two weeks ago, he and three of his associates visited Freddie Johnson's pub, the Queens Arms in Battersea Park Road. Tony and his boys sauntered into the bar and opened fire with a sawn-off shotgun, scattering punters in all directions. None of the Johnson's was present. After the attack, they drove to Freddie Johnson's
house in Bolingbroke Grove, Battersea. And blew out his front windows with the shotgun and sped off back to Fulham.

Sitting down opposite he asks Tony, 'What the fuck is going on, why the hell didn't you
consult with me first?'

Tony drains his glass before responding. When he did, it was like a low rumble of thunder, 'We needed to act fast, we needed to show those wankers, we're not fucking mugs.'

Albert keeping his voice down adds, 'I don't need fucking gang warfare to break out on the streets of West

London. Do you follow me?'

Tony grinding his teeth in annoyance, jolts his head forward. The hairs on the back of his neck spiking, his powerful shoulders straining the seams of his white Polo shirt. Albert is controlling and Tony doesn't like it. When people met Tony, they feared him without even talking to him. He stands at six-four, has deep-set eyes, a broad flat nose and a six-inch scar across his left cheek. When Tony got angry, he transformed into a brutal monster. Having never had moral boundaries, his instinct for cruelty made people respect him and fear him. He has the swagger of someone you don't even want to lock eyes with, let alone cross.

The rival gang, the Johnson's protected Brian Flynn a property developer, formerly from the Elephant and Castle. Albert and Flynn have clashed on and off for many years. Flynn's known to have had links with the IRA in the 80s and is a law unto himself in South London. Flynn paid the Johnson's well. He also used Freddie Franks, who headed up a gang in the Elephant and Castle on occasions, to defend his empire. To the annoyance of the Johnson's.

Albert tells Tony, 'I'm not having it, I pay you well, keep me informed, do I make myself clear?'

Growling he responds, 'Let's get one thing clear Albert, you may pay me well, but don't tell me what to fucking do. Do I make, myself clear?'

Albert, seeking to calm him, 'I'm not telling you what to do Tony. We have a good thing going here, and I don't want to fuck it up.'

Tony spent a lot of time looking over his shoulder and never had remorse for the crimes he'd committed. Or lives he destroyed. He often wondered why he couldn't visualise himself as an old man. It was probably because he was never destined to be an old man.

CHAPTER
20

Luca's about to leave the station to meet Franco for a beer, when DS John Barker approaches him, 'I have some news on the guy you were asking about, Albert Mason?'

'What have you got, John?'

'We've had two local villains, Tony and Danny Daniels under surveillance for two months. PC Pete Docherty logged two days ago, Tony Daniels had a meeting in a boozer the other night, with your very own Albert Mason.'

'Any idea what it was about?'

'No, but there's been two recent incidents involving the Daniel's and the Johnson brothers. The first one in Hammersmith, the second in Battersea.'

'Over what?'

'Again, we're not sure, possibly turf wars.'

'Could you keep me informed if you hear anything else, John?'

'No problem.'

When Luca arrives at Gianni's, Franco's waiting outside, 'I can't believe you're ready, has the restaurant gone bust?'

Franco smiles, 'Come on, I need a pint.'

Leaving the restaurant, they are walking towards the Old Brompton Road, when Luca's mobile rings, 'Hello, Luca Rossi.' No one responds, Luca hangs up and looks over at Franco, 'That's the second time that's happened today.'

Entering the pub, the punters look older than they are,

a man hunched on the bar holding an empty pint glass. A woman crying in the corner, her sobs lost in the racket and din of the bar.

From the bar, someone calls out, 'Franco.'

Franco looking to his left, replies, 'Hello Billy, how are you?'

Everyone in South Kensington knew Billy James. He was the old man who sat in the pub's corner, from opening time until he was drunk. He'd then stagger off home. An ornate pub inside and out it still has the character that predates the modern pubs of today. Glimmering lamps are reflecting on the polished wooden bar, brass rails and opaque frosted glass doors adorn the main bar. Luca cherished London pubs, particularly the conversations that go on in them. He loved the way the punters had a few pints and thought they were experts on everything. Standing with a beer in their hand, talking utter tosh, about a diverse range of topics. The Kings Head is no different.

Getting their drinks, they sit down at a small table. Luca declares, 'I needed to talk to you away from the restaurant.'

Taking a sip of his pint, Franco replies, 'Sounds serious, what's on your mind?'

'Albert Mason, that's what's on my bloody mind.'

Screwing up his face, Franco, squints his eyes and sighs, 'I asked Martina about him yesterday, she bit my head off and told me to stay out of her business.'

'That's unlike Martina, especially to you.'

Franco tells him, 'It's like he's got a hold on her, I don't like it.'

'Earlier today I had a conversation with one of our sergeants at the station. He informed me, Mason recently had a meeting with the head of a well-known crime family, based in Fulham.'

Every muscle on Franco's face tightens, his eyes narrowing, 'Do you know what it was about?'

'No, but I guarantee it won't be about his charity work.'

Franco asks, 'Why don't you have a word with her?'

'She will close up on me and tell me to butt out, as she did with you. I need to come from a different angle. I need to find out more on Mason and what he's up to.'

Franco grins, 'Your right, brother, come on drink up. How is it going with Julia?'

'Definitely on the up, but I have a suspicion something else is going on.'

'What do you mean. Do you think there's someone else on the scene?

'No nothing like that, I think somethings wrong with her health-wise. I can sense it in her eyes. When we were at Bishops Park on Sunday with the girls, I heard Darcy asking her if she was going to the hospital the next day.'

Franco replies, 'Martina might know something, they're still close you know?'

'I know, Martina tells me what she can. Anyway, I hope to find out more. We're meeting at the Bluebird in Kings Road to have another chat.'

CHAPTER
21

No matter what a selfish, deceitful action Albert Mason had taken in his life. He'd never struggled with shame. He's a man who demands to be in control and have things his way, and he would do whatever it took to get it. A towering swashbuckling figure throughout his life. Albert's talkative, gregarious, insensitive, and demands complete allegiance from his friends, family and employees. At one end of the self-loving spectrum, he's a charismatic leader with an abundance of charm. But his grandiosity soars to such heights, it makes him manipulative and easily angered. Especially when he didn't receive the recognition he considers his birthright. He's never followed the rules because he thinks he's too good to abide by anyone's standards. In his mind, he's the exception to the rule. To Albert, he's not even breaking the rules; they never apply to him.
Albert's more than happy to point out to people what they're doing wrong, or enlighten them about something he knows nothing about. Continually reminding them of their faults, so they remain weak while he grows stronger.

From a child, he'd only ever loved himself; he thought he was the best at whatever he did even if he was rubbish at it. Throughout his business career, he'd take credit for other people's efforts, by merely being their boss or having minimal input. Ultimately, everybody's world revolved around Albert's and no one else's.

Arriving for a meeting at his headquarters in Long Lane, Covent Garden at 1.45 pm. He waltzes in through the huge glass doors of the offices and doesn't acknowledge anyone in the reception. Vaulting the staircase, two at a time he enters the main office. Oozing confidence he hurtles into the boardroom like he's on day release from Barbaria.

In the boardroom, he could be the most accomplished diplomat, putting everybody at ease and drawing them in. Today was not one of those days. As soon as he enters the room, the atmosphere changes from light-hearted to tense. Pacing back and forth he turns to face the ten-people sitting around the boardroom table. Baring his teeth in a poisonous smile, he raises his hand and crashes it down hard onto the highly polished wooden table. The attendee's sitting around the table jump with shock. Without a word of welcome or the utterance of an agenda, he rants non-stop for ten minutes. Anxiety and fear grip the management team, who are sitting around the table like wet washing on a cold, windless day.

For hurting people's emotions and feelings, someone had thrown away the key where Albert was concerned. Stopping his ranting, he concentrates his attention on Amanda Flannigan, the in-house accountant. Feeling anxious and breathless as though someone's choking her. She wants to curl up in a ball and wait for someone to save her. But no one would. With his eyes quivering in their sockets, rage builds within him. Exploding, Amanda feels the full force. Bellowing across the room, he tells everyone about the irritations he's suffering regarding her performance, 'What do you think you're fucking playing at?' He roars.

Amanda's heart rate kicks up another notch, looking down she glares at the blank notepaper in front of her. Stepping forward, he snatches the pad from the table and hurls it across the room, striking a window, spreading its blank pages everywhere.

He snarls, 'Look at me when I'm bloody talking to you.'

But she doesn't take her eyes off the desk in front of her and pretends no one else is in the room. In a split second, Albert calms down and is all smiles. The staff have seen it all before and are used to his vitriolic abuse. But, his minions are faithful to him; they say nothing and carry on as usual.

In Albert's world, emotions are the things that make us human. He tells people, you can have happiness, pride and excitement. But where would you be if you didn't feel hurt, pain and despair? He's a bully who can't deal with stress with grace. So, he attacks, no matter who it is in front of him.

CHAPTER
22

Sitting at traffic lights at the top of Kensington Church Street, Martina's thinking about her relationship with Albert, and where it's going. She'd met up with him many times, but never at his home. She knew she had feelings for him but felt something was missing. She noticed he changed when he was in other people's company, as though he was putting on a show. He was enigmatic and people around him appeared to like him. But on occasions, they acted as though they feared him as well. He was so corporate and unbending, Martina had never seen him relax in the time they'd been together. She could never picture him as a toddler or a teenager.

Smiling to herself she reflects, 'I bet he was born in a suit.'

Nothing was colourful with Albert or even grey. It all appeared so black and white with him. When in Albert's company her head rotated faster than a spin dryer. He could be everything, from confident to funny, he was so different from other men she had dated. But nothing ever seemed to add up with him. On their first date, he told her he was an only child. On another occasion, he spoke of a younger brother called Jack. Part of her wanted to walk away, but something fascinated her about him. She's determined to get answers tonight, before committing herself any further.

She pulls up in her Range Rover outside Albert's house at 8 pm. Being part of the Borough of Kensington and Chelsea, Notting Hill Gate is one of the most affluent places to live in London. It attracts a diverse mix of people, including celebrities, bankers and professionals. The detached Georgian house is striking and is set back behind stunning landscaped gardens. He'd previously boasted to her; it had ten bedrooms and ten bathrooms. The mansion is proudly looming behind black ornate iron gates, chandeliers are twinkling in its windows. Edged by rows of trees, swaying gently to the warm summer night breeze, it's got more security gadgets than a military base.

She's about to buzz the intercom when the large black gates open wide.

Shearing across the gravel drive, the car comes to a halt in front of a large bay window. In the middle of the drive stands a delicate marble fountain, it's soft gurgling melodic sound resonating in the surrounding silence. Taking her lipstick from her bag, she paints her lips red and exits her car. Reaching her lower thighs, her dress is clinging to her body, in a way that is elegant and feminine.

Albert opening the front door, beckons, 'Enter my lady.'
She laughs, 'Why thank you, kind sir.'

Dressed in navy blue chinos and a long-sleeved white Polo shirt, Martina comments, 'Blimey no suit, looking casual at last. You look like an accountant on his day off.' Not amused at her observations, he guides her through the hall into the huge lounge. Filled with a Georgian ambience the room's furnished to impress, with fine antiquities, paintings and gilded mirrors. On the left side of the room is an enormous, ornate white marble mantelpiece. Beautiful French windows are looking out on to the gardens, to the side of the house.

As the evening goes on, the atmosphere changes for the worse. Albert may be dressed casually, but there's nothing casual about his face or his demeanour. It's as though he's always on guard like he trusted no one, including Martina. It makes her wonder if it's all a facade, and he's less honourable than she first thought.

Albert summons her to the dining room. Filling the centre of the room is a large mahogany table. In the table's centre, there are two immense silver candlesticks, which hold tall, smooth white candles, whose wax has never dripped. The room is exquisite. The walls are painted pastel blue, and the ceiling is pure white. The French doors leading to the back garden are ajar and letting in the Jasmin scented evening air. All that's missing is the food.

Martina jumps, when she hears a croaky voice from behind, 'Would you like me to serve dinner, Mr Mason?'

Turning she gazes at the elderly woman before her. The ancient woman looks like she has one foot in the grave already. But despite her frail appearance, she appears to be resisting it, every step of the way. Her hair is pure white, her age-spots giving her skin a coffee-stained look. Her jowls are hanging down below her chin.

Albert replies, 'Yes, that would be good Alice.'

The old lady leaves the dining room, her gait unsteady.

With eyes wide open, Martina asks, 'Where did you get her from?'

Albert snubs her remark, 'Dinner won't be long.'

Five minutes later the old woman returns and serves the starter of prawn's marinara. Martina asks her, 'Have you worked for Albert, long, Alice?'

The old lady is about to answer when Albert shrieks at her, 'You can go back to the kitchen now Alice.'

The old lady looks at Martina with tearful eyes, bows her head and totters out of the room, to the sanctuary of the kitchen. After they'd finished their starters, Albert

gets up from his chair and goes to the kitchen. Martina can hear raised muffled voices. She hears the old lady shouting back at him and Albert, raising his voice even higher.
Reappearing back in the dining room, Albert is carrying the main course of steak.
Slamming it down in front of Martina, he sits down and says nothing.

Looking up at him, her eyes wide and angry, she asks, 'Well, what's wrong with you?'

She adds, 'I can see you're angry about something, what is it?'

Ignoring her, he carries on eating like it's going out of fashion. Ramming in the steak, chewing it loudly, treating Martina to views of partially masticated food. Carrying on gulping down the food without breathing, his slurping noises would have embarrassed a pig. Martina has dined with Albert many times, and his manners had been impeccable. Astonished; she's eating hers like it's poisoned, each forkful smaller than you'd feed a baby. Sitting opposite her glum faced, Albert's acting like a cantankerous teenager, staring at her with cold stillness. At that moment Albert's actions had extinguished any sparkle in their relationship. It seemed so much fun at the start, but she knew this was the end of the road for her and Albert.
Feeling a creeping uneasiness, she makes an excuse to leave. Telling him, she has a migraine and needs to go home. Staying silent, still glaring at her, his wide eyes scowl at her. She moves her eyes lower, scanning the floor, not raising them to his eye level. When she does speak, her voice is quiet, with a meekness that is not part of her usual speech pattern, attempting to conceal how concerned she is.

Standing, soaring above her, he roars, 'What the fuck is up with you?'

Shifting uneasily, not sure how to respond, she tries to regulate her voice to keep control, 'I have a headache, that's all.'

Feeling nervous flickering's pricking her chest, she shakes. With a hard fist of fear growing in her stomach, her moist eyes widen and the hairs on her neck bristle. Her heart is racing; all she wants to do is curl up and hide.

Opening a property magazine that's on the table by the side of her, she flips through it and pretends she's not frightened out of her wits. Snatching it from her grasp, he flings it across the room.

'Are you listening, I'm fucking talking to you.'

Not looking up at him. He roars at her again, 'You snotty cow, get up.'

As she stands, he paces forward and thrusts her up against the wall, peering at her with his large bulbous eyes. Sweat is saturating her skin, and her hearts thudding against her chest. She doesn't recall ever being scared like this in her entire life. Pushing him away, she's walking towards the door, when a loud bang makes her cower. Standing up, she can see the flying vase has dented the wall, to her right-hand side. Turning to face him, she sees him launching a china ballerina figurine at her. She crouches, as it slams against the wall above her head, bursting into hundreds of tiny fragments.

Even though he's aware of where she's going, he screams at her, 'Where the fuck are you going?'

They both turn as they hear the dining-room door creak. Appearing in the doorway, the old lady is watching them. Martina's eyes dart around the room, looking for a way out. Seeing her chance, she snatches her bag and runs for the front door. Opening the door, she leaves the house, and a refreshing sweet breeze hits her full in the face. AS she fumbles in her bag for her car keys. The flicker of a lamp makes her jump. Now sitting in the car, she's shaking like a leaf in a hurricane. The world is quiet around her, except for the pounding of her heart and her ever-quickening breath. Starting the car, she heads towards the gates. Relieved when they open, she's trembling and does not want to go home, so she heads for Julia's flat in Fulham.

CHAPTER
23

When Martina leaves Julia's at 6 am the next morning, the air is fresh and invigorating. Sitting in her car outside Julia's apartment, she squints in the mirror. Looking and feeling dreadful, her face is chalk white, her eyes dark and her mouth dry. Driving off for her shift at the restaurant, fear thoughts are still looping around her head.

Thankful for Julia's company, they'd talked into the early hours of the morning, laughing until they cried and crying until they laughed. Not only about Martina's situation with Albert but also Julia's with Luca. Julia was so much more than a sister-in-law to Martina. Julia was a friend who she could rely on, no matter what. She liked to have Julia's unique perspective on situations and could talk to her about personal stuff. Knowing she would get it better than anyone else.

Reaching the restaurant, she sees Marie opening the main door, 'Hi Martina, are you ok, you look pale.' Raising her eyebrows, she asks, 'Did you and Albert have a late night?'

'I'm fine. What time is Franco coming in?'

'He said he would be here about ten.'

Putting on her work shoes in the kitchen, Marie sees Reg at the back window, beckoning her to let him in, 'Hello Reg, how are you this morning?'

Reg, saying little as usual, 'Ok thanks.' He then disappears down the cellar steps.

Martina and Marie are busy in the kitchen when they hear someone thumping on the front door. Martina leaves the kitchen and enters the central part of the restaurant to see what's going on; when she sees Albert grinning through the glass of the front door — holding a large bunch of flowers in his hand.

Her legs to go weak and her stomach twists. She screams at him, 'Go away you bastard. I don't want you near me.'

Ignoring her, he rattles the door handle trying to get in. Martina, realises she hasn't locked the door and Albert bounds in, 'All by yourself, are you?'

'No, I'm not.'

'Look, I only want to talk to you; don't worry, I'm not going to hurt you.'

As he advances towards her, a scream from deep within forces its way from her mouth, 'Get away from me, don't come near me, you fucking animal.'

Holding out his hands, he tries to reason with her, 'I'm sorry about last night, it was all a misunderstanding, that's all.'

Marie comes tearing out of the kitchen to see what the commotion is about.

Martina shouts at her, 'Phone Luca, now.'

Marie takes her mobile from her apron. Before she can use it, Albert rushes over to her and snatches it from her grasp, slamming it to the floor.

Turning, he advances towards Martina and clutches her by both arms. Trying to pull free she slips, and gravity brings her down with a thump on her back. Scrambling to get back up her legs move from under her like she's on ice.

Finally getting to her feet, she retreats backwards towards the kitchen, with Marie following behind. As they reach the kitchen door, Reg strolls out bearing a massive rusty ball pane hammer by his side. Pushing past Marie and Martina, he stands in front of them, glaring at Albert.

Albert stops in his tracks, as Reg holds the hammer above his head, scowling at Albert.

Albert bawls at him, 'This is fuck all to do with you, you freak, get out of the way.'

Reg hisses, 'Come any closer, and I'll shatter your brains, and rip off your face.'

Breathing, heavily Albert's hands ball into fists. Lost for words, he sees sense and backs off. Shaking his index finger at all three of them, tells them 'You haven't seen the last of me, and I mean all of you. You don't know who you're fucking with.'

Embarrassed and shaken, he turns and leaves the restaurant, kicking chairs and tables as he goes.

Trembling, Martina looks up at Reg, 'Thanks so much Reg, the man's a maniac.' Reg turns and without uttering a word returns to the cellar.

Putting her arms around Martina, Marie asks, 'What the hell was that all about?'

With her watery eyes enlarging, she tells her, 'As you know, I went to his house last night for dinner. Things were fine at the start, but as the night went on, he turned nasty and terrified the life out of me. He was yelling so loud at me it seemed like the walls were shaking. At one point, his face was crimson, and it looked like his eyes would pop out. With spit dripping from his mouth; he leaned in closer and grabbed my face with one hand, holding the other aloft, glowering at me with his evil eyes. If it wasn't for the old lady who had served dinner coming in, God knows what would have happened.'

'The man sounds like a lunatic; I told you he had cold eyes.'

Marie adds, 'Are you going to tell Franco and Luca?'

'You bet I am.'

CHAPTER 24

Arriving at the Bluebird restaurant in Kings Road, at 12 pm, he finds Julia's already sitting at a table pondering the specials, on the chalkboard menu. His heart slams at the sight of her. Putting a hand on her shoulder in a possessive gesture, he kisses her on the cheek. Her smile broadening in approval.

Julia asks, 'Have you spoken to Martina today?'

'No, why do you ask?'

'She stayed at my flat last night.'

'Both pissed again?'

'No, she went to Albert's for dinner, and he terrified the life out of her.'

'What?'

'He turned nasty on her.'

Luca fumes, 'What, he hit her?'

'No, but at one time she felt he was about to, but she managed to get out. You should talk to her yourself.'

'Oh, I will. I've had my suspicions about Mason. Was she ok when she left your place?'

'Yes, she seemed fine. She left at 6 am and went straight to the restaurant, for her shift.'

Luca changing the subject, 'Anyway enough about that, how are you?'

'I'm fine.'

'What about the girls? I can't wait to see them at the weekend. Are they looking forward to it?'

'Yes, they are. They're happy with everything at the moment, they keep talking about our trip to Bishops Park last Sunday. I even heard Darcy telling the neighbours about it before she went to school this morning.'

A waiter, with his small touch screen computer in hand, approaches to take their orders. After placing them, Luca gets straight to the point, 'You say you're fine, but you're not, are you?'

'What do you mean?' Knowing full well what he meant.

'I'm concerned, I know something's amiss, and I know when you're withholding something from me.'

Tears tremble on her eyelids 'You can still read me like a book, can't you?'

'Yes, I can, come on tell me. What's wrong?'

Her defences subside, and she reaches out for his hand, 'I have Multiple Sclerosis.'

Luca's heart almost stops in shock at her words. His shoulders stoop and he takes in quick,
shallow breaths. With knots, forming in his gut, his face turns to stone, 'I don't know what to say, I'm so sorry.'

He adds, 'Have you kept this to yourself?

'Yes, I've not told anyone, including Martina.'

Luca's voice now thick with distress tells her, 'When we met in Fulham Broadway, I knew something was wrong. Why didn't you tell me then?'

'I wanted them to be wrong. I couldn't expect you or anyone else to understand, when I hadn't accepted it myself?'

'How long have you known for?'

With tears dripping down her face, she tells him, 'Two months.'

'How have you been coping with it?'

'My memory and thought process has gone haywire, and my walking is a lot slower, mainly because I'm unsteady on my feet. I'm exhausted most days, but other than that.' She frowns and smiles, 'I'm fine.'

When the waiter brings over their meals, they've both

lost their appetites. Picking at their pasta's they don't finish them. Luca tells her, 'We can't talk here, come back to mine, and we can talk more?' Julia agrees, and they leave.

Entering the hallway of Luca's house, the first thing Julia notices is the framed photo of herself and the girls, on the hall table. Luca's making tea in the kitchen when she hears his mobile ringing, 'What is it?'
Rick is on the other end, 'Can you talk?'
'No, not now, Rick, I'll call you later.'
Hearing the phone shutting down, Luca enters with two mugs of tea. Handing Julia's, hers he sits down on the sofa next to her. They talk at length for over two hours about Julia's illness, the children and the situation they are both in. They also reminisce about when they first met and how they fell in love. Over a few short months. She tells him, 'After we met that first night, it felt as though my heart was dancing around my chest, it went on for days.'
He tells her, 'When I first saw you that night in the Whitehorse, there was something even then. It was like you cast a spell on me, there and then. I've never been the same person since.'
After a pause, he adds, 'How did it come to this Julia?'
Reaching for her face, he tenderly kisses her. His kindness, quality and aroma trigger an explosion of hormones, within Julia. Gazing into her sparkling eyes, he grasps her delicate wrist and leads her to the bedroom. Her heart's pounding at his nearness, enjoying the rippling of excitement, ripping through her body. Standing by the bed, she puts her arms around his neck and presses her wet plump lips to his. Kissing open mouthed panting, their bodies work together. Feeling

sparks of static dancing over her skin, Luca unzips the back of her white dress. Slipping it off, it crumples to the floor, next to her bare feet. Unbuttoning his shirt, sends delicious shivers of want, through her body. As Luca slides the straps of her white lacy bra from her shoulders, she gasps handfuls of his hair, her nails raking his scalp. Luca resumes undressing her, his fingers grazing over her body. Feeling his rugged hands, it gives her a sense of protection mixed with ecstasy. Gently laying her down on the bed he moves his mouth downwards, his kisses slow and wet on her slender throat. Kissing his way across her bare skin, their bodies melt into each other. Luca couldn't recall a time when he didn't love Julia. And now her love is bringing him back to life, in ways he could never imagine.

It's over a year since Julia had felt that magical feeling; it makes her shudder with pleasure and delight.

Sensing Luca's hot breath in her ear, he tells her, 'I love you, I have missed you so much.'

Her eyelids flutter like a newborn butterfly, as contentment fills her. Flashing him a knowing smile she whispers in his ear, the words he'd yearned for, 'I love you so much, Luca Rossi. I never want to lose you again.'

At this point, he feels he's the happiest man in the world. Julia smiles at him as they sink back against the pillows, both laughing with breathless stuttered sounds of happiness.

Entering the bedroom after her shower, she disposes of the white towel adorning her head, sending her blonde hair tumbling into the small of her back. Luca who is still laying on the bed, his legs outstretched before him, Observes Julia dropping the towel that's draped around her, to the floor. She steps across the room to a chair, picking up her white knickers, and steps into them. Clipping up her hair, taking on the sexy secretary role, she beams a smile at Luca. With his eyes caressing her, a sheen of sweat is shining above his upper lip. He tells her, 'I want to rip those off, and start all over again.'

Grinning, she tells him, 'I would, but I've got to pick up the girls.'

In the hallway, they kiss and say their goodbyes and agree to talk later that evening.

When Luca switches on his mobile, it beeps five times. He thinks to himself, 'Here we go again.' He's about to listen to the messages, when the phone buzzes, its Rick, there's been another murder.

CHAPTER
25

Driving to the murder scene in Lena Gardens, Hammersmith, Luca exhales a deep sigh of satisfaction, sensing a renewed energy. He can't believe what had happened earlier that afternoon, and can't keep the grin off his face.

Reaching the scene, Sam is standing outside the imposing red bricked, bay windowed Victorian house. As he opens his mouth to speak, Rick appears at the top of the steps and beckons them to ascend the steps, to the front door.

Informing them, 'It's the same MO.'

Luca enquires, 'Are you certain?'

'Yes, in every detail, one hundred percent.'

Putting on their white protective clothing, they enter the house. Luca can see the property is devoid of any furniture or belongings of any kind.

Sam tells him, 'A neighbour told me, it's been empty since the last tenants moved out, over six months ago. She also told me the builders, finished the refurbishment two weeks ago.'

Luca follows Rick and Sam through to the dining room, at the rear of the property. The horror that confronts him takes Luca's breath away. He's now seen this carnage, three times in the last few weeks. Each time the scene in front of him hitting him harder. The killer has left girl's naked body, face up spread-eagled across the floor. Looking as though she's in her early twenties, she has a well-rounded figure and long blond hair.

Sam informs him, 'We have discovered her ID. Her name is Sophie Flynn. Her driving licence shows she lived in Parliament View Apartments, on the Albert Embankment.

Two hours ago, Luca had been making love to Julia in his bed. His euphoria for what transpired earlier, now suppressed. Rick is right; the scene is a carbon copy of the other two murders. The girl is laying like a slaughtered animal, in a pool of her own blood, her white skin stretched tight against the bones of her face. With no eyelids, she's staring blood-spattered murder at Luca, forever. At this moment Luca's living in another world, a world of despair and suffering.

It's always the same, body's icy cold, the life that had lived within them gone. Limbs at awkward angles and heads, held in such a way they can't be sleeping. Only abandoned shells left to decay.

Blood is everywhere, and the coppery smell of it is invading his nostrils, leaving a metallic taste in his mouth.

Sam asks him, 'What do you make of it, boss?'

Luca doesn't answer and carries on staring at the horror in front of him. He had seen many dead bodies in his years in the force, and death was routine to him. But these murders were off the scale. He tells Rick to finish and leaves the scene with Sam, and they head to the dead girl's address.

'Do you know where this address is boss?'

'Yes, I'm sure I've been to the block before, a few years ago. It's on the south side of Lambeth Bridge.'

'Sounds grand.'

Arriving at the address, the low dazzling circle of the early evening sun is glinting across the Thames, above Vauxhall Bridge. It dawns on Luca why the address is familiar.

He tells Sam, 'It's just come to me. I know Sophie Flynn's father; his name is Brian. He's a known criminal; supposed property developer turned straight. I questioned him about a vicious assault that took place in a pub in Lillie Road, over two years ago. We knew he was guilty, but no one would talk. Including his victim, who had forty stitches inserted into his face. Sam presses the buzzer on the entrance wall, a few moments later a man answers, 'Is that Brian Flynn?'

'Yes, it is, who wants to know?'

'It's the police, Mr Flynn. We need to talk to you.'

Under his breath, Sam hears Flynn mutter, 'For fuck's sake, what now?'

The door opens, and they enter the reception area. Taking the lift to the penthouse apartment. The ultra-modern elevator glides its way to the top, within a matter of seconds. The lift door opening, straight into the hall of Flynn's apartment. Brian Flynn is standing in front of the door, clutching half a glass of whiskey, staring into it like he was watching a television show. With no greeting, he turns his back, and they follow him into the open-planned lounge. It's luxurious; the vast space has floor to ceiling windows, allowing plenty of light to flow into the room. Spectacular views are permeating throughout, including the Houses of Parliament and the London Eye.

Flynn has a two-day stubble and is sporting a blue pin-striped suit. The kind you only see solicitors and villain's wearing. Expressionless, his grey, cold eyes settle on Luca. Flynn is of a sturdy build and stands around the six-foot mark and appears to be in his late fifties. Supporting a head of steel grey hair, his eyes are narrow, giving him an agonised expression. He has an East End accent and the swagger of a person you wouldn't want to mess with.

Flynn, giving an impatient shrug of his shoulders, asks, 'Well, what have I done now?'

'It's not about you Mr Flynn; it's about your daughter Sophie.'

Sam interjects, 'Earlier today someone discovered the body of a girl, at an address in Hammersmith. I'm sorry to tell you Mr Flynn, it's your daughter Sophie.'

As Sam's words overwhelm him, Flynn's face is intense but motionless. Collapsing back onto the brown leather sofa behind him. His tears are flowing unchecked; his skin has turned grey, making it look thick and leathery. Sitting in the chair, with no will to move, he murmurs, 'My baby, my baby.'

The shock has carved merciless lines into Flynn's face.

Luca asks, 'When did you last see Sophie Mr Flynn?'

With his face cupped in his hands, he replies, 'Yesterday morning when she left for work. I didn't stay here last night. I've only been in for an hour. What happened to her?'

'She's been murdered Mr Flynn.'

Sam asks, 'Where did she work?'

Sobbing he tells her, 'She worked for me, part-time at my office in Sloane Square.'

Luca despises the likes of Flynn, but it's hard to pull their world apart when it involves their children. They continue to question Flynn for more than half an hour. Luca makes a mental note of Flynn, mentioning the word revenge at least three times in the last five minutes of their conversation. They stop when Flynn starts to become agitated and aggressive.

As they are leaving, Luca asks Sam, 'Can you drop me off back at my car in Fulham, I need to go to the restaurant to meet Franco? I'll see you tomorrow.'

It's 9 pm when Luca arrives at Gianni's. As he enters Franco, calls out, 'Sit down, I'll bring you over an espresso, we need to talk.'

Luca looks over at Martina, who is behind the counter

serving a customer. Looking up at him embarrassed, she waves, giving him an uncomfortable look.

When Franco joins him at the table, Luca tells him, 'Julia told me about Martina and Mason, what the fuck is going on?'

Sitting like a coiled spring waiting to snap, Franco, keeping his voice down replies, 'The man's a psycho, he turned on Martina for no reason last night. He then came bursting into here, first thing this morning when I was out. She's petrified of him; he's phoned her three times already today.'

Luca asks, 'What did she tell you?'

'Only that he was shouting and bawling at her, launching his prized ornaments at her head. She told me this morning. She wouldn't go near him again.'

With bulging eyes, Franco adds, 'But I will, I'm going to fucking annihilate him.'

'No, don't go near him, leave it. I'll deal with it, I promise.'

'I hope you do it fast brother, or you will be arresting me.'

He leaves Franco to find Martina. Finding her in the kitchen, sitting at a table crying, Reg is sat opposite her. Reg gets up as Luca approaches.

'Thanks for helping Martina earlier today Reg, Franco's told me what went on earlier this morning.'

Reg nods and half smiles but says nothing. As he's walking away, Martina calls over to him, 'Please don't do anything Reg? Let us deal with it.'

Reg leaves the kitchen, shutting the back door behind him.

Luca asks, 'What was that all about?'

'He overheard me telling Franco what took place at Mason's house, last night.'

'We all need to calm down, I've told Franco I will sort it, are you ok with that sis?'

Martina nods, telling Luca, 'I've told him it's over, and I want nothing more to do with him.'

'Taking aside what took place last night, has he acted like this before or is it the first time it's happened?'

Tears well in her eyes, 'Over the last few weeks he's been acting strange. But last night he took it to another level. As soon as I arrived at the house, I could feel the atmosphere was tense.'

She adds, 'When he started on me, I could see rage and hatred in his eyes. His face was as dark as a storm cloud, every time I opened my mouth, he got angrier. At one point, I thought his eyes were going pop out. They were protruding so much.'

Luca tells her, 'Over the last few weeks we've been having a close look at him. I can't say too much, but we know he's engaged in criminal activities on a significant scale all over London. We've also been talking with people associated with him in the past They told us he surrounds himself with supportive friends and allies, but gives them nothing back. And from what they've told us, he seems to have a single-minded focus on how to destroy people.'

He adds, 'Having met him at the V&A, I get the impression, he's controlling and deems everyone beneath him.'

Martina frowns and tells Luca, 'I can believe all of that.'

Putting his arm around her, pecking her on the cheek, he tells her 'Come on cheer up sis, it's not your fault. But promise me one thing, if he turns up here or at your flat, call me straight away.' Martina nods and smiles.

CHAPTER
26

Entering Luca's office, Sam and Rick see him, lost in his thoughts, Sam asks, 'Are you, ok boss?'

'Family trouble that's all Sam, nothing to worry about, sit down.'

Luca continues, 'I'm getting a lot of pressure from upstairs, we need a result fast. What have we got on the latest murder?'

Rick pulls the beige folder he's holding, from under his arm and hands it to Luca, 'Again boss, there was no murder weapon left. The only evidence was small pieces of a latex glove, on the floor around the body. And they don't match the gloves used by the first responders.

Something flashes beneath the surface of Luca's hardened expression, 'That sounds promising.'

Sam tells him, 'We've sent over to forensics.'

Rick continues, 'Her killer left her bag, credit cards, and jewellery at the scene. So again, we can forget robbery as a motive. He also cut the same body parts from her. On this occasion, neatly stacking them on a work surface in the kitchen.'

Sam adds, 'One of the resident's in Lena Gardens told us she sighted a man loitering outside her house, on the day of the murder. She described him as very tall and dark, but that's all.'

Luca had been here before. Most cases went through this phase; nothing fitted together even though your gut told you it should. All you needed was time to let the fragments fall together. But he knew they were nowhere near cracking this one.

Rick, grunts, 'We need more help on this one, boss. We

need to get it out there.'

Luca holding his right hand to his right temple examines the reports. He tells them, 'I agree with you Rick. Yesterday I sat in a meeting upstairs, where some of our so-called superiors told me they didn't want to create panic. I told them I didn't agree with them and we need the help of the public. But for the time being, they want us to keep it under wraps, for as long as we can.'

'So, what's the plan?' asks Sam.

'We go over everything again and leave nothing unturned. If this killer is not caught, he will continue to offend. He will become even more empowered and feel he'll never get caught.'

He adds, 'These types of killers plan their crimes more than other criminals. They take time to select their target and dispose of their victims. As we know, this is difficult and the logistics involved complicated. Especially when there are multiple sites involved as we have here. Over the years I've interviewed a few serial killers. They're usually arrogant and have an inflated sense of importance. Much like narcissists, they think the usual rules don't apply to them. They have grandiose ideas about their potential. They believe they deserve to be the boss and convinced they are the best at everything they do. They can come across as delightful people and are great at making small talk, their quick wit drawing people into them. They usually have fascinating stories and convincing tales to characterise them in a favourable, and believable light. So, let's keep this firmly in our minds.'

Rick, mumbles 'Or they could be just a complete fucking head case.'

Leaving the office alone Luca heads, for Albert Mason's office in Covent Garden.

CHAPTER
27

On his way, over to Albert's office in Covent Garden, Luca thinks about how he's going approach the subject of Martina. Being a personal matter and not police business, he needs to be cautious. Luca's Merc enters Albert's office car park, tyres crunching in the dusty gravel. Sitting in his car checking his messages, it hits him, like a light switching on in his head and recalling his conversation with John Barker at the station. John had told him there had been trouble between the Johnson brothers and the Daniels brothers in Battersea and Hammersmith. The Johnson's protected the interests of Bryan Flynn, and Flynn is a business rival of Albert's. Luca also knew Tony and Danny Daniels looked after Albert's business interests. And now Flynn's daughter is dead. Could there be a connection, was it that simple?

Breezing into the bustling reception of Albert's office he approaches the reception desk. The receptionist has a bored look of a middle-aged woman, gone to seed. Her sallow skin ageing her beyond her years, 'I need to see Albert Mason could you let him know Luca Rossi is here?'

Peering over the top of her glasses, in a surly voice, she asks, 'Do you have an appointment Mr Rossi?'

'No, I don't, but I am certain he will see me, call him now, please.'

Sitting down, he picks up a magazine from the small table beside him and flicks through it, not looking at anything in particular. Within seconds, a tiny woman wearing shiny black shoes and a pearl necklace, appears at the side of him, 'Mr Rossi, would you like to follow me, please?'

At the top of the stairs, the woman shows him into a large open plan office.
Spotting Luca entering, the staff stop reading their internet pages and glare at him.

'Mr Mason is concluding his meeting. He will be with you in a few minutes.'

'Listening to the sounds of the office, he can see Albert through a glass petition, conducting his meeting. Albert's standing, addressing a group of twelve people, who are sitting around a large boardroom table. From what Luca can see and hear, he's giving them an unwanted lecture. Albert's doing all the talking with an air of authority and the appearance of someone who demanded obedience. Five minutes later the meeting breaks up. Whatever it was about, Luca could tell by the attendee's faces; it hadn't gone well.

Striding out of the meeting he heads in Luca's direction, 'Luca what an unexpected pleasure.' His smile is without humour, 'Let's go to my office.'

Albert's office is a large room occupying the corner of the building. Having floor-to-ceiling windows, it's giving magnificent views across Covent Garden. Sitting on his mahogany desk is a laptop, a notebook and a stack of papers lying under a massive glass paperweight.

'Please take a seat, Luca. Would you like a drink?'

Ignoring both comments, Luca continues standing. Sitting down at his desk, Albert gazes down at a piece of yellow notepaper in front of him. Putting a flourishing signature on the bottom, he pushes it to one side. Drumming his fingers on the desk, he looks up grinning and asks, 'So Luca, how can I help you?'

With his pulse rising, he gives Albert a penetrating look, 'You know full well, why I'm here.'

Albert not supplying the desired reaction replies, smirking, 'I don't, is it official?'

Luca roars back, 'No, it's fucking personal.'

Albert twists in his chair, returning a piercing gaze. Albert only saw people that were ordinary, inadequate and worthless, 'So, how can I help you, my friend.'

'You can help by staying away from my sister for a start. And let's get it straight, I'm not your fucking friend.'

Trying to intimidate Luca, Albert stands, walks towards him and looms over him. There's a pause as he glares at Luca. Luca beams back, both sets of eyes, unblinking. Albert sneers, 'Has she told you about our dinner date? It was nothing, a misunderstanding that's all, nothing else.'

Luca's never backed down in his life. With pulse-pounding assurance, he moves closer to Albert, 'Believe me, Mason, there's no misunderstanding where I'm concerned. Stay away from my sister.'

Albert, grimaces, clenching his jaw so tight Luca thinks his teeth are about to crack into a thousand pieces. Albert visualises his fist slamming into Luca's nose, splattering blood across all four walls of his office.

Rubbing his fingers across his dry lips he bawls at Luca, 'Another thing, you can tell that skinny freak that works at your restaurant to back off, threatening me with a hammer was a big mistake.'

Probing for information, Luca stares back at him, 'There's one more thing, how well do you know Bryan Flynn and the Daniels brothers?'

Albert's voice sounding abrasive and husky tells him, 'I'm assuming you know the answer to that question already. So, why ask?'

Luca can see a concerned look on Albert's face. With a contemptuous grin, tells him, 'Just asking, that's all.'

Luca's words wrangle in Albert's mind, his eyes widening before narrowing, his knuckles white from his clenching fists, he tells Luca, 'I have another meeting in five minutes and six urgent calls to return. Is there anything else?'

Seeing Albert's cheeks turning red with anger, 'For now, yes.'

Burning rage is hissing through Albert's body, as Luca turns and leaves the office. Reaching the car park, Luca looks up he sees Albert at a window, glaring down at him. Leaving the car park, he parks the car in a side street and calls Sam. He tells her to get everything she can on Mason and Flynn including any business dealings they've had over the past ten years.

CHAPTER
28

Vic and Charlie Johnson are well-known residents of Battersea and cousins of notorious South London gangsters, Dave and Tommy Gibson, who reside in Camberwell. In their younger days, Vic and Charlie Johnson headed a gang which accepted battles with other groups across South London. In those days, Dave and Tommy Gibson were part of Johnson's mob. The last two years have seen the Johnson's and Gibson's become close again. Their reunion taking place after a rival gang from Peckham attacked Charlie Johnson with axes and baseball bats when he was leaving a pub in Vauxhall. The Gibson's helped the Johnson's take revenge on the rival gang from Brixton. Now having pooled their violent talents, they are now the most powerful gang in South London.

Leaving their scrap metal yard in Bagleys Lane at 10.30 pm. Tony Daniels and five of his crew, including his brother Danny, head through the shadowy back streets of Fulham towards Wandsworth Bridge. Thirty minutes later, entering Queenstown Road, Battersea, they pull up in the stolen black BMW 4x4. Just shy of the Falcon Club. No one says a word; there's just silence. With shadows now dissolving into the night, the alleys and street corners are in darkness. The feeble light of a nearby flickering neon strip, from a minicab office offers little light. It's no Italian Plaza in springtime.
Tony nods and all six of them exit the car. Strolling to the back of the BMW, Tony opens the boot. Danny is at the front of the queue and has the first choice of the weapons laying on the black carpet of the boot. Without

hesitating, he picks up the well worn sawn-off shotgun and a box of cartridges. The rest of the gang follow picking up various weapons, comprising of a machete, iron bar and pickaxe handles. With a fight involving the Daniel's, there's no honour, no code. What counted was the winning, and Tony Daniel's took nothing for granted. Opposite the club, Tony spots a dishevelled figure, hunched over beneath the crumbling doorway of an old boarded up sweet shop. He concludes it's just someone sleeping rough. There's no one else in sight.

Tony and Danny had visited the club before, so knew the layout well. With steady footsteps, the six of them draw closer to the drab looking club. Reaching the entrance, Tony who's leading from the front lays his hand on the door. Looking at the other five behind him, he counts the beats of his heart, waiting until he senses the moment is right.

He takes in a deep breath through his teeth, 'Come on, lets fucking do this.'

There's no smoking ban in the Falcon; it works within the Johnson's rule book. The club's thick with smoke that's forming twists in the gloom. The harsh odour of alcohol and smoke hitting them as they enter. The first thing Danny hears is Frank Sinatra, belting out 'That's Life' on the sound system. In Tony's way is a bleached blond, tarty looking woman, struggling to keep her balance. He pushes past her and she swears at him. Tony sneers at her, 'Piss off, you drunken old bitch.'

Its wall to wall people, most of them drinking in silence, hoping that the answer lies at the bottom of their glass. Others are in drunken slurred nonsensical conversations. Guided by Tony, they move forward pushing people, chairs and tables out of their path. Tony's eyes dart from side to side taking in everything in front of him, he spots Vic Johnson at the bar surrounded by a crowd of people. Vic Johnson looks older than his actual age, years of drinking and smoking robbing him of his youth.

In the frozen second between standoff and fighting, Vic Johnson's eyes flick from the man standing beside him, to Tony. Tony's face is indecipherable; he has no fear. If hatred were visible, the air between them would be scarlet. Tony advances on Vic Johnson and his associates standing at the bar. The men standing beside Vic Johnson push the women standing with them to one side, leaving both mobs standing and staring at each other. Vic Johnson steps out in front of the men surrounding him. With the club now almost empty, he bellows at Tony, 'What the fuck do you want Daniels?'

Without another word said, all hell breaks loose. Tony fronts Vic Johnson and throws his weight behind a right-hander. With blood spurting from his nose Vic Johnson falls in slow motion to the floor. Tony grabs him by the collar, lifting him to his feet. A crack echoes across the bar as Tony knees him in the face. He continues battering Vic until he collapses to the floor. Standing behind Tony, Danny takes the shotgun from under his leather jacket and fires. The single shot rents the air, belching smoke and fire, annihilating the optics behind the 1950s style bar. Tony's gang stand opposite Johnson's group wielding machetes and iron bars. Johnson's mob knows full well they can't compete and back away, leaving Vic Johnson helpless spread out on his back, bleeding from his face.

Danny yells at him, 'I'm going to blow your fucking kneecaps off Johnson.' Taking a step back, he points the gun at Vic's legs.

Vic looks up at him, smirking, 'You haven't got the

bottle you prick.'

Without batting an eyelid, Danny pulls the trigger. The shotgun roars, the pellets raking red revenge, blowing away Vic Johnson's right kneecap, like a magic trick. A chill sweeps down Vic's spine and his stomach aches, as pain jolts through his body. Blood bubbles up from the wound and his arms and legs lose tension, weakening his body from head to toe.

Danny's startled when a woman comes from his left-hand side, scraping her red fingernails down his cheek, clawing for his eyes. Stepping back, he gives her a backhander across the face, sending her crashing to the floor. One of Johnson's associates, Pete Timmins launches a wooden table at Danny, but it has no impact. He then lunges at Danny with a right hook but misses. Danny jabs out his hairy fist, seizing his wrist, breaking it. He then smashes his elbow into Timmins nose, spreading it across his face, sending him sprawling across the blood stained wooden floor. Timmins is about to get to his feet when Tommy Hurren makes a ruin of his arm with an axe, covering everyone standing nearby in a shower of blood.

Leaving a pathway of broken beer glasses, bottles and furniture across the floor. Tony and his boys exit the club, leaving it looking like a tornado had ripped through it. They're approaching the 4x4 when a black Audi A4 screeches to a stop in front. It's Johnson's reinforcements. There are four of them, two armed with hammers, one with a baseball bat, the other is bearing a 12-inch zombie knife.

A large black man bearing a hammer runs towards Danny, Tommy stepping forward, lands a punch making the man's head snap back like a balloon in the wind. Tony orders his boys to get in the car; they can't afford to get involved in another battle in the full glare of the public.

The other gang are now surrounding the BMW. A huge man dressed in a green bomber jacket strikes the front passenger door with a baseball bat. Another tries to smash the window screen with a hammer. As the 4x4 screeches away, another man carrying a machete finds himself wedged between the 4x4 and a lamppost. Tony screams at Tommy Hurren as the BMW stalls. Tommy turning the ignition key, the engine explodes into life. Thundering away, the 4x4 sprays dirt and dust into the warm night air. On the Chelsea side of the bridge, they turn left onto Cheyne Walk; the tyres screeching in protest.

Passing the houseboats on their left, the lights are shining on the black River Thames. Turning left into Lots Road. They stop halfway down by a telephone box and park up behind Danny's royal blue S Type Jag. Danny, Tony and three others get into the Jag and roar off, back to the scrapyard in Bagleys Lane. Tommy Hurren remaining in the driver's seat of the 4x4 follows behind, but turns off and heads to a field near Heathrow Airport, where he will set the 4x4 ablaze as planned. Arriving at the scrapyard, Billy Montgomery exits the car and opens the gates. The royal blue Jag, shrouded in silver moonlight enters the yard and stops by three parked vehicles, on the right-hand side.

Standing in the yard hemmed in by tall stacks of scrapped vehicles. Looking austere, composed and pleased with himself, Tony tells them to make sure their alibis are solid. They agree to meet in the Queens the following evening at 8 pm. Two minutes later, the Jag and the three other cars leave the yard heading to different parts of West London.

CHAPTER
29

Arriving at headquarters at 7.30 am, Luca notes a buzz about the place. Everybody seems involved in hushed conversations. Walking through the reception, the desk sergeant calls over to him, 'John Barker was looking for you a few minutes ago. He needs to talk to you.'

Sitting down at his desk, he's about to call John when there's a tap on the door and John Barker enters the room, 'What have you got John?'

'A shooting over in Battersea last night guv, at the Falcon club in Queenstown Road. We've had officers over there most of the night. The word is it involved the Daniels and the Johnson's. Vic Johnson had a kneecap blown off, and Pete Timmins had his left arm almost severed by an axe. They're both in the Chelsea and Westminster Hospital, under armed guard.'

Luca smiles, 'And I bet no one saw a thing?'

'Spot on guv.'

'Can you get the reports to me as soon as they come in? I think it's time we visited the Daniels.'

As John Barker leaves the room, Rick appears, 'You've heard the latest then?'

'Yes, get a car; let's pay them a visit.'

Driving to Tony Daniels scrap metal yard in Fulham, Rick muses, 'It's funny, whenever anyone mentions a scrap metal yard. The TV programme The Sweeney comes to mind. I can't stop myself picturing villains fighting amongst stacks of battered Vauxhall Viva's and Ford Cortina's.'

Luca laughs, 'I wonder if they've fed someone into the crusher today.'

Turning left, into Bagleys Lane, they pull up outside the graffiti splashed gates of the scrapyard. Rick's a big man and has a voice which could break windows at one hundred yards. Thriving on this part of the job, he's never intimidated. Passing through the gates, from the right-hand side of the enormous yard, dogs bark and growl, tugging at their leashes. In another corner smoke ascends into the clear blue sky, giving off a smell of burning wire. In front of them a crane is stacking cars and scrap metal high, making metallic structures, that resemble towering buildings. Luca spots the office, a shack of a building on the left-hand side. Two blue plastic chemical toilets are standing to its right hand side. Outside the office Luca spots a man in a dark suit, handing over a wad of cash to another man dressed in dark blue overalls. When the man in the suit spots Luca and Rick approaching, he gets into his silver Lexus and drives off towards the gates. The car's tyres, blowing red dust across the yard.

Shattered glass is crunching under their feet as they walk towards the office. Without knocking, they bound into the ramshackle office. The stench of alcohol and sour sweat hang heavy in the air. Sitting at a tea stained wooden desk, Tony Daniels is sitting alone. He might have been handsome once upon a time, but his features now ruined by a flat nose. Giving his face a somewhat flattened appearance, as though he'd angered someone, brandishing a large frying pan. With two-day stubble decorating his jaw, he looks every inch a gangster.

Tony looking up, grunts, 'What do you want, Rossi?'

Luca grins, 'Not sure Tony, have you visited Battersea lately?'

Smiling, gulping his tea from his greased stained Chelsea mug, 'No, can't stand the place, full of fucking dogs and funfairs.'

Rick growling like a pit bull, 'We heard you took a trip over there last night with some friends?'

'Must be a mistake, I was in the Norfolk Arms all night. Ask the governor, Roy Knight; he will vouch for me, and my brother.'

Getting straight to the point Luca asks, 'What's your relationship with Albert Mason?'

'I've known Albert for years. He's an acquaintance that's all. We both grew up around here in Bagleys Lane. Someone told me you lived around this part of the world too?'

After Luca and Rick depart the yard, Tony leaves his office and stands outside the gates of the yard. Gazing up and down Bagleys Lane, Tony's face has a granite hardness, his bare arms more ink than skin. With his blonde hair cropped, from a distance he could be mistaken for being bald. These are the streets Tony grew up on, the streets he'd walked his whole life. He knew them as though someone had engraved them into his head, with a blunt knife. Raising his head skywards, he blows smoke from his lips and stamps out his cigarette on the hot cracked pavement.

Tony was born in William Parnell House, which sits towards the end of Bagleys Lane, in 1962. One of seven children he had a tough upbringing. His father's family were well-known market traders in the area. Leaving school aged 14, he went straight to work for his father Lenny, who was a third-generation stallholder in the North End Road Market. It was Tony who kept the stall profitable, as Lenny's drunkenness was the rule, rather than the exception — spending most of his working day in the Norfolk Arms, drinking and playing cards.

His brother Danny approaches from behind, cleaning his fingernails with a knife. The same knife he sank into a man's eye a week ago. People were saying failure to pay up provoked the assault. Danny asks, 'You ok?'

'Just had the old bill in, asking questions about the ruck in Battersea last night.'

'Do you think they're on to us?'

'Yes, but no one will talk.'

The brothers now feel they're about to hit the big time. And the yard is to be their business front, for their more lucrative criminal enterprises.

Tapping Tony on the shoulder, he beckons Danny to follow him, 'I want to show you something.'

Danny had had a thing about guns, the way they felt, the power they had and the carnage they caused. Entering a dilapidated building at the back of the yard. Danny moves a rusty metal cabinet away from the wall. Bending down, Danny removes a wooden panel on the rotting floor. Reaching in, he pulls out a rolled up in a piece of oily rag. Unfolding it, he hands Tony a pristine, Belgian-made semi-automatic pistol. Focusing his attention on the gun, Tony weighs it in his hand, finding the balance between himself and the weapon, 'It's got a good balance, a snug fit and its compact.'

Smiling, Tony asks, 'Where did you get it from?'

'Our usual supplier, I've got another nine down there and another ten on order.'

Tony enquires, 'Where are you going to offload them?'

Danny replies with a grin, 'The usual place, our friends south of the river.'

CHAPTER
30

After checking out Tony and Danny Daniels alibis in the Norfolk Arms, Luca asks Rick to drop him off at the Bedford pub in Dawes Road.

Rick asks, 'Do you think there's a link between Mason, Flynn, Daniels and the dead girls?'

Luca replies, 'To be honest Rick, I'm not sure, it's a bloody puzzle at the moment.'

Pulling up outside the Bedford Arms, Luca tells Rick, 'I'll see you back at the nick later.'

Cutting through the Aintree Estate, he had only one thing on his mind; he wants to see Julia. Five minutes later, reaching her flat, he knocks on the door. After thirty seconds, he knocks again but there's still no answer. He's thinking to himself he'd had a wasted trip, he hears Julia calling out, 'Hold on, I'm getting there.'

Bending down on one knee, peeping through the letter-box he sees Julia tottering along the hallway, holding onto the wall. Seeing her struggling to get to the door, he tells her, 'Take your time, there's no rush.'

Opening the door, she falls into his arms, 'This bloody MS. Sorry I'm so slow at the moment.'

'Don't apologise, come on let's get you into the lounge and sit you down.'

With, Julia sitting on the sofa he goes to the kitchen and makes two coffees. Then re-joins her in the lounge.

She tells him, 'I think I'm going through a relapse at the moment and there's not much I can do about it.'

'Do you want me to pick up the girls for you this afternoon?'

'No, it's fine. My neighbour Naomi is picking them up.'

Sitting opposite, not knowing what to do to, he feels helpless.

She tells him, 'I've noticed I don't bounce back as quick as I used to when first diagnosed. As much I try to keep it at bay, I think it's winning the war.'

'Have you been able to get out with your friends at all?'

With her lips trembling, she tells him, 'Yes and I enjoy going out with them, but on the last two occasions, I found it difficult. I'm now avoiding going out altogether, which makes me worse. Sometimes the preparation is just too much, so I end up staying at home. I don't know what will happen next week, let alone in the future. That's the thing I find most worrying. Not knowing what the future holds, especially where it concerns the girls.'

'It's so upsetting to see you dealing with this on your own. I want to be there for you, to love and care for you.'

Tears fall from her frightened eyes, 'I never wished to put this on you, Luca,'

He tells her, 'I love you more than anything in this world, Julia. If I could, I'd take this off you right this second. You know that.'

He adds, 'You must get so lonely?'

'If I'm having a bad day, after taking the girls to school, I come home and rest on the sofa. Reading books and watching daytime TV. Over the last few months, I've realised who my true friends are. People say they meant to call; they've been thinking of me but didn't want to bother me, in case I'm resting. What hurts the most though, are people who never call. The ones who've slipped out of sight altogether.'

'I miss you so much Julia, to hell with the rest of the world and their attitudes. I want you back.'

She sobs as Luca adds, 'We should be together, I miss

those big sparkling blue eyes of yours and that smile.'

Happiness fills her, her tired eyes smiling at him, she tells him, 'I love you, Luca Rossi.'

Touching her face, gently wiping away her tears, he brings his lips down onto hers. A small breathless whisper, escaping his lips, 'I love you so much.'

Julia's feels a renewed spirit, as they continue talking about Julia and the girl's moving into Luca's house in Parsons Green Lane.

CHAPTER
31

Having found out about the battle at the Falcon Club between the Daniels and the Johnsons, Albert's not concerned. He wishes to put some more work the Daniel's way and requires their full cooperation. Parking up opposite the club, he arrives at the Queens pub in Bagleys Lane at 3 pm. He's about to get out of his Bentley, when his mobile buzzes, 'Hello, Mason speaking.'

There's silence, but he knows someone's on the other end. It's the third time it's happened this week. Exiting the car, lightning flashes and slashes across the dark sky above him— his towering ungainly figure bounds across the road, a torrent of rain hitting him before he gets to the entrance.

A young boy in white shorts and a blue Chelsea shirt is standing outside the club peering through one of its grimy windows. When the boy sees Albert, he puts his hands in his pockets and spits, trying to act tough and impress Albert, 'Can I look after your car, mister?'

Smiling, Albert inquires, 'How much is that going to cost me?'

'A pound, mister, that's all.'

'Make sure you guard it with your life, and I'll give you two.' The boy's blue eyes bulge.

Sauntering into the pub, pairs of eyes from all sides, look in his direction. The pub is seedy and dimly lit, but if you looked hard, you could make out the black and white photos of British boxer's, covering all four walls. Albert watches a busty blonde gyrating around a brass pole in her bra and knickers in the centre of the floor. He hears Danny's laugh ringing out, with a note of childish merriment, from the far end of the bar. It's an infectious laugh and it's the first detail to catch Albert's attention, other than the busty blond.

Spotting Tony and Danny sitting at a table to the right-hand side of the bar by a window, looking out onto the drenched street. Danny sees Albert approaching and calls out in his gravelly voice, 'Albert you look wetter than a mermaid's minge. What do you want to drink my old son?'

'A double scotch would be nice, Danny.'

Danny asks, 'What do you think of our stripper Albert?'

Albert snarls, 'She's so fucking ugly a sniper wouldn't take her out.'

Danny laughs, 'She's got a fanny like a ripped-out fireplace.'

Danny is the younger of the brothers. Around West London, he's known as a complete head case. Recently discharged from prison, after serving four years for assault, he's also known for his harsh handling of the women in his life.

Tony growls at Albert, 'I hope you're not going to have a go about our ruck with the Johnson's in the Falcon Club, the other night?'

'No, that's your business Tony. It's not an issue with me.'

'Well, you've changed your fucking tune.'

At that point, Danny returns with two pints of lager and a double scotch.

Placing the drinks on the table he grins at Albert, 'I hear Brian Flynn's not a happy paddy? Someone's mullered his minders and his daughter's brown bread, poor bloke.'

Albert ignores his remarks, takes a mouthful of his

scotch and swills it around in his mouth before swallowing it, 'I've got work for you two.'

Tony sits forward, 'Sounds good Albert, is it a good earner?'

'Yes, I need someone sorted in Fulham but I don't want to talk about it here. I want it completed in the next few days. I'll be in touch with the details tomorrow.'

Albert, gets off the subject, 'It's quiet in here today.'

Danny raises his glass and beams, 'Chelsea must be at home?'

Albert enquires, 'I've heard rumours you two are turning into arms dealers?'

Albert smirks and takes another sip of his scotch. Tony and Danny both look at each other, surprised. Laughing Tony, enquires, 'Where did you hear that?'

'I know everything Tony. They say you've got more guns than Davy Crockett at an arms sale.'

Tony wants to smash Albert into oblivion there and then, but plays it cool.

'We've heard it all before Albert, just rumours that's all.'

Albert smiles, nods and sips his scotch, 'If you say so, Danny.'

'I do Albert.'

Albert breaks the awkward silence, 'So what is going to happen next in the Johnson saga?'

Tony chirps up, 'Thought you weren't going to mention that?'

Albert snaps back, 'There will be repercussions you know?'

Danny replies, 'There will be no comebacks, mark my words.'

'It's not the Johnsons you should be wary of; they have friends.'

Danny declares, 'No one worries us Albert, we've got it covered.'

Albert downing the rest of his scotch, stands, 'Well boys I'll be in contact tomorrow.' He then leaves.

When he gets outside, a refreshing breeze blows through his hair and strokes his craggy face. The clouds have disappeared and with it the rain. Nearing the Bentley, he sees the rugged little boy in the Chelsea shirt standing by the passenger door, 'The cars all ok, mister.'

'What's your name?'

'Billy Daniels.'

'Are you Tony's son?'

'No, he's my uncle, my dad is Danny, but I live with my mum in Stephendale Road.'

From his pocket, Albert pulls out a roll of notes and bungs him a crisp tenner, 'Here you go, Billy.'

'Wow thanks, mister.'

Albert gets into his car, with a self-satisfied smile on his face and drives off into the bright sunshine, back to Notting Hill Gate.

CHAPTER
32

Sitting at his desk in the half-light of his office, Luca's browsing through reports. Rick taps on the door and enters, 'Do you want some good news boss?'

Luca sighs, 'I could do with some Rick, what have you got?'

'We've had a good look into the business dealings of Bryan Flynn, as you requested.'

'Please tell me they involve Albert Mason?'

'We found plenty on Mason's dealings with Flynn, but we went deeper. Sam suggested we had a look at all three of the murdered girl's fathers. And what do you know? We found Mason has had links with all of them.'

'What sort of dealings?'

'Not joint ventures, it's mainly legal disputes, to do with land and property around the London area.'

'Brilliant, we might be onto something. Can you put a summary together and let me have it as soon as possible?'

'Sam's doing it now.'

Rick adds, 'Do you think Mason is capable of these murders? There must be more to it than getting pissed off about some business dealings?'

'I can't see it, but stranger things have happened.'

Rick shakes his head, 'Whoever is doing this, their hate must be so profound. Fair enough, a nail in a tyre, a scratch on the paintwork or abusive phone calls, but not this.

Luca muses, 'Maybe the killer enjoys it? He may like the power, thrill and lust. Or is it revenge? A serial killer keeps killing until one of three things happens he's caught, he dies, or he burns out. The way he kills and leaves the girls at the scene is a signature: a ritual, something he does for emotional fulfilment. Serial killers pose their victims in certain ways or leave them in a specific place, after killing them. Another signature might be a method of torture or mutilation. It's what the killer does to fulfil his fantasies, and it can tell us about his personality. I know we are missing something here.'

He adds, 'We define a serial killer as one who murders three or more victims, with cooling-off periods between each murder. This sets them apart from mass murderers who kill four or more people together, or in a short time in the same place. Serial killers work alone, kill strangers and kill for the sake of killing as opposed to crimes of passion?'

Sam enters the office carrying a pile of files. Placing them on Luca's desk, she tells him, 'I've found five court cases spread over the last ten years involving Mason and the fathers of the three girls. The cases involved millions of pounds and Mason has lost the lot.'

Luca smiles, 'Great work Sam. We have something here we can work with.

'Can you look closer at Mason's dealings with the father of Eve Thomas. Rick, you have a look at his dealings with Robert Lane. I will look at his dealings with Brian Flynn.'

CHAPTER
33

Late Sunday morning Luca pulls his car to a halt outside Julia's flat. Amalee, Darcy and Julia are waiting outside the entrance of the mansion block, in the bright sunshine. Screaming with delight Amalee and Darcy run to him. Scooping them up in his arms, he swings them around. After hugs and kisses, they head to Gianni's for lunch. The first few minutes of the journey are silent. Luca looks over at Julia, and thinks to himself she looks tense; her features suspended between sadness and bliss. But it's not silent for long, as the girls sitting in the back, break out in uncontrollable laughter, filling the car with beautiful sounds. The sounds Luca's missed so much over the last twelve months. Amalee is so excited about the prospect of going to Gianni's, asking her to sit still is like trying to tell a fire not to burn. Her every muscle needs to move and jump.

Luca's mind drifts back to the Saturday afternoon, when they told the girls to sit down and that they needed to talk to them about something important. Amalee thought it was about holiday plans. Luca and Julia told the girls that things would never be the same again. He recalls his beautiful daughters bursting into tears and sobbing their hearts out, for what seemed an eternity. Julia told Luca after the separation Darcy became distressed most mornings when she dropped her off at school. Amalee had a different reaction. She had trouble sleeping and gave up all interest in playing with friends.

Luca still feels inadequate regarding his daughter's futures. He recognises there will be a mixture of behavioural and emotional issues for them ongoing if he and Julia do not get back together. Luca knew it was common for children to have difficulties distinguishing fantasy from reality, as they try to make sense of what is going on around them. He didn't want them developing ideas which frightened them and made them sad. He didn't want them thinking he didn't love them anymore or the breakup was because of their behaviour, or anything else they might have done.

Parking the car outside the restaurant, he leans across and kisses Julia on the cheek, short and sweet. Getting out of the vehicle, Darcy shouts, 'Hold my hand daddy and grips onto him as she would never let him go.'

He'd often told Julia stories his mother and father told him when they lived in Italy. The 50s and early 60s were difficult times in Italy; they were still feeling the effects of the war. In the post-war years, there were no luxury foods on the table; most family's just consuming pasta and soups. His father Gianni believed Sunday lunch was a tradition worthy of respect. Something Luca's has carried with him since a child.

They are just about to enter the restaurant when Luca's mobile rings, and he immediately regrets answering it, 'Hello, Luca Rossi speaking.'

A croaky voice on the other end, tells him, 'Stay away from Albert Mason, or you and your family will fucking regret it.' The caller hangs up.

Looking over at Luca, Julia, raises her eyes, 'Work?'

Luca smiles, 'No, just a wrong number, that's all.'

Entering the restaurant, amazing smells hover in the surrounding air. Luca picks up the rich combination of garlic, tomatoes, bread and the earthy almost narcotic aroma of truffles, sliced extravagantly over plates of spaghetti. This is Luca's idea of heaven. The girls adore

Martina and run to meet her like a drove of stampeding elephants. Martina greets them and as usual and makes a big fuss. Martina shows them to a table set for them in the restaurant's corner. Wine glasses are sparkling on the bleached white tablecloths, and carafes of red wine are filled to the brim. Much of Italian life revolves around the family dinner table. It's where family bonds are forged and roots of love and friendship developed. If Italians know how to do one thing, it is how to make memories around a dinner table. They understand and appreciate the magical synergy created by the joy of conversation and intimacy when mingled with the pleasures of beautiful food and drink.

Striding over, Franco puts his arms around Julia, telling her with tears in his eyes 'It's fantastic to see all you guys together again.'

Luca's missed moments like these more than anything. Looking over at Julia, she's laughing with the girls, looking so happy. He thinks to himself; he was paying a small price compared to what she's going through with their breakup and her MS.

Luca asks Franco, 'I take it you and Martina are going join us?'

'We wouldn't miss this for the world.'

The meal went on into the late afternoon, everyone talking, eating and laughing. Julia's face was an epic picture of pure happiness. Looking at his beautiful family, Luca thinks to himself, 'Things will only get better from here.' He was to be very wrong.

An Italian journalist once wrote 'In the heart of every man, wherever he is born, whatever his education and tastes, there is one small corner which is Italian.'

Luca's dream of going to live in Italy with his family is still at the forefront of his mind. It's a lifestyle that easily

seduces those living in harassed, time-pressured cities like London. The Italian way of life, with an emphasis on doing things slowly, appeals to him, like the perfect dream.
He's snapped out of that dream when he remembers the anonymous phone call. Making his excuses, he leaves the table to call Rick to ask him to put a trace on the call.

CHAPTER
34

After his shift at the V&A, Reg is wandering along Exhibition Road in the early evening sunshine, when his thoughts turn to Martina. She's brought brightness into his world — something he'd never known in his life. As a child, his father abused him both physically and mentally. Horrifying images of his childhood still plunder his head, just as they've done throughout his life.
He remembers his father beating him mercilessly; Reg, with tears rolling down his face screaming. His mother yelling for his father to stop, his father shouting back, 'Shut up; it's the only way to teach him.'

Reg would yell at him, 'Stop, I won't do it again dad. I promise, please mum make him stop.'

Most of his adult life he's had a reoccurring nightmare, and it's always the same. He wakes up in a strange hospital, surrounding him are bright white lights and barren, sterile white walls. A nurse with long blonde hair down to her waist, and red lipstick smudged all over her face is gazing down at him. His father is standing behind the nurse holding his belt aloft. His father and the nurse get close, then further away and then closer again. He's desperately screaming for help, but nobody comes.
Over many years, he's kept his sadness inside and pulled away from everybody, which has made him isolated. In his teenage years, he became aggressive, and it drove people even further away. His negative feelings coupled with his continued seclusion has led to depression, throughout his adult life. Feeling rejected and lonely for most of his life, it's now permanently damaged his self-esteem beyond repair. Being dissimilar to everybody else

wasn't that bad for him, it's the ridicule he couldn't take. Following the death of his mother ten years ago, he's now alone in the world. Often, he'd shuffle around the streets in the middle of the night not sure if he was dead or alive.

Entering the gloomy house something's making him nervous. It could be the tinge of the wrong aroma, but something feels wrong. He's startled when he hears a gruff voice, 'Hello, Reg. We've been told you've upset a good friend of ours.'

Standing in the dim light opposite him, he sees two men, then a third emerging out of the gloom behind him, closing off all prospect of escape. Terrified, he freezes solid. Tommy Hurren is a five-star violent bully, who would batter the crap out of anybody for saying boo to him. Any provocation no matter how insignificant, his temper would blow. He was a titan of a man, with a large head, enormous ears and a thick powerful neck. Striding forward he throws his body weight behind a right-hander, smashing Reg on the left side of the jaw — sending him reeling backwards. Drawing his arm back again, Tommy drives his fist into Reg's nose. Bracing the heel of his boot against the threadbare carpet, Reg raises his arms as shields to protect himself, awaiting further blows. Ronnie Oliver laughs after his fist connects with Reg's face. The force of the blow, splitting the skin over his left cheekbone. Reg shrieks with pain and drops to his knees. His mouth erupts in pain, tasting blood pooling in his mouth. The toecap of Tommy's boot connects with his rib cage sending Reg rolling over. Holding his side in agony, he calls for help, but nothing comes out of his mouth. Closing his eyes, forgetting about the world, the three of them lay into him.

After they leave, immobile on the floor his skin pale and

cold, he tries to get up but realises its futile. His bloodied body is quivering as his consciousness ebbs in and out. Searing eruptions of pain are pulsating around him, increasing with each movement he makes. Oozing out of his face is a slow but persistent flow of crimson. Laying there, he's never felt more alone in his life. With the help of a chair, he rises to his feet, sending pain amplifying through his body. Retrieving the mobile in the pocket of his brown overalls, he dials 999.

CHAPTER
35

Martina's busy tidying tables after the morning rush when Franco, waving the phone, calls over to her, 'It's the Chelsea and Westminster Hospital, asking for you.'

Grabbing the phone, 'Hello, Martina Rossi speaking?'

Hi, Martina 'My name is Julie Adams. I'm calling from the Chelsea and Westminster Hospital. Reg Grimes has asked me to call you. We admitted him to the hospital last night.'

'What's wrong with him?'

'Three men violently assaulted him at his house when he returned from work last night.'

'My God, how bad is he? Is he ok?'

'We are still checking him out, so it's hard to say at the moment. But it's not life-threatening.'

'Can you tell him I'm on my way, what ward is he in?'

'He's in Douglas Ward. I will let him know you are on the way.'

Arriving at the hospital ambulances, are lining up in a long queue, at a side entrance. Entering through the large automatic sliding glass doors, she sees a child wailing in its mother's arms. Another woman, short of breath and gasping for air, telling a nurse she's been waiting for over five hours.

Looking up she scans, blue plastic signs showing the specific areas of the hospital and its wards. Nowhere is the chronic underfunding more evident than in the hospital's corridors. Crammed with patients on trolleys, some tended by strained relatives, and some alone. The busy hospital is stifling and has an undertone of bleach throughout, coupled with an antiseptic odour.

The walls are magnolia, scraped from the hundreds of trolleys that have slammed into them. Nurses are rushing with a calm devotion on their rounds. Martina spots an elderly woman lying down in bed, her thin bones pressing against her skin. The apparatus around her keeping her alive. The old lady's eyes catch Martina's. Martina can see the desire and fire in the old lady's eyes have gone; just her hollow soul is reflecting in her tear-stained eyes.

Reaching the Douglas Ward, Martina asks a nurse where Reg is. She points to a bed at the end of the ward. Surrounding the bed, a curtain hangs limply on a chrome railing. Pulling it back, she's shocked, hardly recognising Reg. He's a mess, his nose smashed and both cheeks swollen. A TV set hangs from a wall. In the corner are two chairs, frayed with wear and tear. It's a typical hospital room, scant and functional. Hearing groans from the adjacent bed, she's glad for the screens around her. It meant she didn't have to engage with whoever was on the other side.

Martina surveys the scene. Bleeping machines are surrounding his bed. Reg has his eyes closed, taking a deep breath, she whispers, 'Reg.'

Raising her voice somewhat, she calls again, 'Reg, can you hear me?'

His eyelids tremble and open. His tired brown eyes are searching. Raising his head, he focuses and mumbles, 'Martina.'

He's awake, but listless, his chest heaving more quickly than it should, trying to bring in more air. Martina smiles warmly, her smile spreading to her eyes, 'Sounds like you've been in the wars, Reg?'

'Something like that.' He closes his eyes and lays his head back on the pillow.

The colour's drained from his face and his hands are twitching involuntarily.
He tries to speak, but only spit drools from his mouth. Martina struggles not to stare at his nose, but her eyes keep switching to it. Spotting purple welts, spread across his abdomen like a disease. It looks like someone's used him as a human punch bag.

Gasping for air he tells her, 'It hurts me to breathe, they're looking at the X-rays to see if I've fractured any of my ribs.'

'Reg, lay back and relax.'

He looks at her with tears in his eyes and then closes them. Holding his hand, she enquires, 'Do you know who did this Reg?' He shakes his head and doesn't answer.

Martina spots a nurse approaching, followed by two policemen. The nurse tells Martina they need to talk to Reg alone, so she leaves.

Fifteen minutes later the two policemen leave the ward and enter the corridor where Martina's sitting, she stands and asks, 'Did he tell you what happened?'

The younger of the policeman tells her, 'He says he remembers opening the front door, going into the lounge and being confronted by three men. But that's it. He recalls nothing else.'

She asks 'Was his mum ok?'

'There was no one else in the house. His neighbour told us he lived in the house alone. Apparently, his mother died over ten years ago.'

The other policeman tells her, 'We will talk to him again later this afternoon.'

Martina knows full well who is responsible for the attack and phones Luca.

CHAPTER 36

Harry Wise, is better known as 'Happy Harry' because of the perpetual scowl on his face. Harry is a professional gambler who enhances his income by taking contract killings. He's known for his extraordinary hand-to-hand combat skills and a penchant for brutality. Over the last ten years, he's murdered seven people for profit and two more for fun. Harry plans his murders with surgical precision, then strikes with the sudden violence of a sledgehammer.

Preserving an unemotional detachment to his victims, he prefers not to think of them. But when he did, it was as if they were already dead. To him, it was like any other job of work but instead of dispatching emails, he dispatches people.

Harry displayed a considerable talent for crime at an early age. With his size and ability to move, it made him formidable. He started his career as a petty criminal and spent his teenage years in and out of borstals. His notoriety increased in his twenties, and it wasn't long before he joined Freddie Coomber's gang in the Elephant and Castle, South London.

Harry would lend money to vulnerable clients, like drug addicts and the needy. When they didn't pay up on time, he would take them to a soundproof room and sadistically torture them. And to this day, he still takes pleasure in damaging people. Some say he foams at the mouth when he carries it out.

Harry is now a natural-born killer and has no qualms about committing brutal murders. Built like a gorilla, but light on his feet, he stands six feet four and weighs sixteen stone.

After a meeting with Brian Flynn a week ago, he's ready. Flynn has paid him well to take revenge for the shooting of Vic Johnson, in the Falcon Club.

Leaving his home in Medlar Street, Camberwell at 3 pm, he heads for Fulham. Harry was born in Stead Street, Walworth, London in 1976 to Maxine and Joseph Wise. His father Joe a well-known criminal in South London, started his career heading a team of bouncers. Who operated the doors of clubs and pubs around the Old Kent Road in the 60s and 70s. In 1984 Joe took part in a £20 million gold heist and was never convicted. Joe also set up a drug smuggling operation from Morocco during the 80s and 90s but is now retired from all criminal activity.

Parking a mile away from Danny Daniels's house in Pearscroft Road, Harry walks the rest of the way, not wanting to get his car caught on any security camera footage. Making his way across Wandsworth Bridge Road, he keeps his head down and eyes straight ahead. Spending the next fifteen minutes walking through the back streets of Fulham, he dodges CCTV, including camera's mounted inside and outside shops. Dressed casually in blue Levi jeans, a navy blue polo shirt and a navy baseball cap and carrying a black and white leather holdall. He looks like he's spent the afternoon at the gym.

It's 5.30 pm as Harry saunters along Bagleys Lane. He's done his homework and knows Danny lives alone and will not arrive back for another hour.

For Harry, most hits were easy. It wasn't like the movies where things get overly complicated. The hardest part was getting his victim isolated. So, once they were dead, he could leave the scene quickly without being spotted.

He knew Danny never locked the side gate to the garden and no alarms were protecting the house. Danny's reputation, keeping any burglars at bay.

Approaching from the side of the property, the gate is rickety and hangs at a jaunty angle. Ivy's cascading over the fence; tendrils are growing in every direction. Passing a small garden fountain, its water is softly gurgling around him. The honeysuckle bushes filling the air with a sweet scent. Taking a crowbar from his leather holdall, gaining entry within seconds, through the French windows. Standing in the centre of the dining room surveying all around him in absolute silence, the place smells like the interior of an old clock. Light is flooding through the gaps in the heavy blue velvet curtains and reflecting off the polished wooden floors. The room is modern, simple and painted white. As he moseys around the house, with murder on his mind, he focuses his attention on the gun he's now holding. Glancing down at the weapon, he has the eyes of a hunter, framed in a loveless face of an assassin. The gun is perfect for despatching Danny. The gun is cold, but within seconds it becomes warm, feeling more like a part of him than a tool of death. Harry holds the pistol in his fist, below shoulder height, primed to pump two rounds into his prey. The second Danny Daniels rears his ugly head.

At 6.35 pm, Danny parks up his black BMW in Pearscroft Road. Waving to a neighbour he crosses the road and enters the house, by the front door. Placing his keys on the hall table, he picks up the letters, spread across the floor. Looking down at the letters, he strides into the lounge, he's stunned when he hears, 'Hello, Danny boy.'

Looking up, he sees the barrel of a gun peering into his soul. Harry's finger curls around the trigger and rattles off two shots in quick succession. Hearing the satisfying thud of suppressed gunfire, the gun muzzle flashes white hot. Danny's dead before the sound of the first shot reaches his ears. A shower of red, rains from his head and paints the white wall behind him. His body slumps down hard like a pile of laundry hitting the floor. Two bullets have torn holes through the front of his forehead. The entry wounds are small, but the exit wounds are a gaping mess. The shots have disposed of most of Danny's brain, via the exit wounds. A short trail of smoke is snaking its way out of the holes in his forehead. The pool of blood around his head is continuing to grow across the polished wooden floor.

Looking at the blood and brain matter on the white wall behind Danny's body, Harry smiles. With the job done, he will be £20,000 richer, for what has been one of the smoothest hits he'd ever performed. With his corruptive grin, he leaves the scene with a display of power and confidence.

CHAPTER
37

Taking a rare afternoon break, Luca's appreciating the open space and fresh air of Hyde Park. It's his piece of heaven, in the urban jungle where he lives and works. Stopping on the Serpentine Bridge, he sees rays of golden sunshine dancing lightly across the lake. The silver blue water is laying without a ripple under the sunlit blue sky. The lake's teeming with life, from the birdsong in the surrounding trees to the sound of fish sucking amongst the pink and white lily-pads at the water's edge. With a deep sense of serenity, his thoughts take him back to the memories of his childhood holidays in Italy. The holidays took place where his father Gianni was born, in the tumbling coastal town of Positano, a cliffside village on southern Italy's Amalfi Coast. Seen from the sea, set in a striking vertical panorama of colours; the green of the Monti Lattari, the white, pink and yellow of the Mediterranean houses. Luca remembers being told stories of Positano by his father and how it's linked to legend. His father told him about sunken boats and treasures in ancient times when Turkish vessels became beached off the shores. One ship carried a painting of the Virgin Mary. The captain heard the painting whispering 'posa, posa' ('set me down, set me down') and obediently threw the painting into the sea. Miraculously, the ship floated. The locals built a Church on the spot where the painting washed ashore — interpreting the episode as a sign that the Virgin Mary had chosen their town as a resting place. Looking out at the lake entrenched in his thoughts, he's fantasising about returning to Italy one day with Julia and the girls and telling his father's stories to his daughters.

On a wooden bench to the left of him, he sees a couple sitting and laughing. Below the table, he can see them holding hands and their feet curled around each other. He recalls the first few months when he met Julia, and they fell in love. How he felt when their hands first touched and their eyes looked into each other's. He knew love came in the strangest forms. Sometimes it stayed, sometimes it walked away. A crushing wave of despair hurts him and hot tears well in his eyes. As he realises, he may never get the only women he has ever loved back in his life.

He's shaken out of his daydreaming when his mobile rings. It's Rick, 'Hi boss, I've got news.'

Luca responds, 'Please, not another murder?'

'Yes, but not what you think. Someone shot Danny Daniels dead at his house in Fulham, last night.'

'Are there any other details?'

'None.'

'OK Rick, I'll see you at the station in thirty minutes.'

CHAPTER
38

Pulling his car up outside the Daniels scrap yard in Bagleys Lane at 2 pm. Albert's getting out when his mobile vibrates, and he answers, 'Mason, speaking.'

No one replies, 'Who the fuck is this?' Still, no one answers, Albert curses again and turns the phone off.

Approaching the gates of the yard a teenage girl, staggers in front of him. The scars on her arms and legs, looking self-inflicted. Regaining her footing, she moves backwards, finding nothing but the crumbling brick wall behind her. Albert's eyes follow her and she smiles at him. Standing at the rusty gates, he finds a written sign on a scrap of brown card stating, 'Closed.' Albert bangs on the gates and dogs bark on the other side. After an eternity, the gates screech open and Tommy Hurren beckons him to come in.

Albert asks, 'How is he?'

'He's had better days.'

The girl who approached Albert outside, pushes past Albert and confronts Tommy, 'Have you got any gear today, Tommy?'

'No, now piss off, I've told you once already this morning.' The young girl walks away with her head bowed.

Albert watches as a crane seizes a car and drops it into the crusher. For a moment, it rests on a pair of shelves. The shelves lift upwards, plunging the vehicle into the trough. The operator, sitting in a glass cabin, presses a button and there's a belch of black smoke. The shelves close in on the car like a giant insect folding in its wings. There's a grinding sound, as it crushes the vehicle until it's not bigger than a roll of carpet. Albert strolls across the squalid yard towards a Portakabin, his gleaming black brogue's gathering dust, to his annoyance. Arriving at the office, he bounds in without knocking. Tony is sitting at his desk with a bottle of Jamesons in one hand and a glass in the other. On the desk, there's a revolver and a box of bullets.

Tony smirks, 'You're the last person I expected to see. Have you come to gloat?'

Albert's about to answer when an insignificant middle-aged, balding man enters the chaotically untidy Portakabin. Wearing fogged up wire-rimmed glasses, he stops, unbuttons his jacket and takes out a handkerchief and wipes the lenses. Holding the glasses to the light, he puts them back on. He looks up at Albert, putting out his hand, he introduces himself, 'Archie Webb.'
Albert doesn't know the man but has heard the name. Before Albert can introduce himself, Tony butts in, 'Archie will find out who had my brother killed.'

Albert, giving Tony a curious look, 'That won't be fucking hard, will it Tony. I told you there would be repercussions. It's clear who did this.'

He adds, 'There again; you've upset so many people, it could be anybody in London.'

Swallowing his drink in one gulp, Danny stands, his chair propelling backwards hitting the wall behind, 'Don't come in here fucking preaching. I want the bastards who did this. And I won't stop until I find them.'

Tony's face distorting with rage, snatches the bottle of Jamesons from the desk, hurling it across the room. Albert ducks as the bottle explodes into hundreds of pieces, hitting the wall to the left side of his head.

Tony roars at Albert, 'Did you know Danny had a son?'

'I did Tony. Billy, I met him outside the Queens a few

days ago when I came to see you.'

Putting both hands down on the desk, 'The poor little mite doesn't even know his dad's dead yet.'

Archie Webb interrupts, 'I'm off now Tony, I will let you know when I find something.' The man scurries across the room and out of the door as quick as his little legs could carry him.

Albert sitting down opposite Tony, shakes his head, 'You need to get your head straight Tony, they will come for you next.'

Tony looks up at him, 'To be honest, I don't give a shit.'

'You don't mean that Tony, I'm serious, you need to get it together. I will see what I can find out. But I guarantee, I will not have to look any further than Flynn.'

Tony asks, 'Do you think he's putting the murder of his daughter down to us?'

'No, I don't, if Flynn thought that you wouldn't be here now. I think it's down to your ruck with the Johnson's.'

'You know I can't just leave it, don't you?'

'I understand that Tony, what I'm saying is get your head together before you do anything. Flynn is a powerful man and will stop at nothing.'

CHAPTER
39

Parking his white van directly outside the entrance of Julia's apartment block in Kingwood Road, he turns off the engine. He sits there with a face of utter indifference as if he were waiting for a bus on a summer's day. Opening the glove box, he reaches in and removes a pair of latex gloves, stuffing them into his coat pocket. Something flashes beneath the surface of his hardened expression, when he sees Julia parking her car behind his van. Adrenaline's courses through his veins, making him feel like every fibre in his body is throbbing in anticipation. Levelling his stony gaze on her, he smiles to himself; the smile is cold and cruel, just like him. He needs to run, to shout, to tell everybody what he was about to do to her, but he had to be patient. His revenge would be her ruin.

Placing down her Marks & Spencer's bag on the floor, Julia rummages around in her handbag, searching for her front door keys. Entering the flat, she places her bags onto the hall floor. Holding on to the hall wall as if her life depended on it, she hobbles into the lounge and slumps on the sofa exhausted. Like most days, her MS has brought on excessive fatigue. It's not just tiredness; it's chronic, debilitating exhaustion. Having an hour before she picks up the girls from school. She lays her head back, closes her eyes, sinking into a deep sleep. There's not a sound as the key turns in the lock; not a sound as the door swings back on its oiled hinges, his dishevelled figure slipping in like a shadow. Closing the door behind him, his steps are as noiseless as a mouse. Spotting her bags in the hallway, he proceeds towards the lounge. Peering through the door, he sees her asleep on the sofa. Drawing closer, he sees her only movement is the slight rise and fall of her stomach. Grinning, his hand runs up her leg, and up to her chest — his gaze drifting up to her pretty face.

His anticipation is a nervous energy, tingling through him like electrical sparks. Having watched and followed her for days, after all his preparations, he feels he'd earned his treat. Loading the syringe from the small brown vial he's holding. A faint smile lightens his brooding face as he plunges it into her thigh. Julia jolts waking, from her deep sleep. Opening her eyes, her body becomes petrified stone when she sees him glaring down at her. Her perception of time distorts, and everything slows around her. Slapping his hand hard across her face, she falls back against the back of the sofa. With blood streaming from her nose; he puts his hands around her neck and squeezes. Her eyes enlarge, her lips part and her world develops into a blur of dull colours. With his face coming closer; she can hear him panting, like an out of breath dog.

Sensing a blackness coming over her like a blanket: not a blanket of warmth, but a blanket of remoteness. The drug is making her eyes heavy. Her thoughts now nonsense, as her consciousness ebbs in and out, dragging her into a dark world of dreams. Baring the facial expression of someone expecting a wonderful gift, he secures her hands and feet. Excitement is threading through his body like he's plugged into the mains, sending appalling thoughts trundling through his head like a train, with no intention of stopping. The killing wasn't his favourite part; it was a necessary task rather than a desire. It was the games he enjoyed most, and he had so many enjoyable ones to play. By the end, they wanted to die. Most times they didn't even raise a hand to defend themselves.

CHAPTER
40

Crossing the busy Brompton Road, Luca's phone buzzes, 'Hello, Luca Rossi speaking.'

'Hello Mr Rossi, this is Miss Foster, the headmistress at Munster Road School.'

'How can I help Miss Foster? Is everything ok?'

'I'm not sure, Mr Rossi, I am calling to let you know that your wife Julia didn't turn up at the school to collect the girl's this afternoon. We still have them here. We've tried to call her several times, but can't get a response, the phone going straight to the answering service. I hope all is ok. Would it be possible for you to come to the school and pick them up as soon as possible?'

With anxiety rising in his body, 'I'll come now, but it will take me at least half an hour to get there, is that ok?'

'That's no problem Mr Rossi, see you thirty minutes.'

Luca calls Sam, explaining the situation, he asks her to meet him on the corner of Brompton Road and Beauchamp Place, as soon as possible. Ten minutes later, Sam's car squeals to a standstill beside Luca, to the annoyance of a London taxi driver, who hoots and hollers obscenities at her. Luca tells Sam to head to Munster Road, Fulham.

Parking outside the school in Bishops Road, they walk at a pace to the main entrance. The corridor is wide, straight and has white walls — not a handprint or scuff mark insight. Posters adorning the walls are advertising school events and after-school clubs. For Sam, something is unsettling and thinks to herself, 'Why do schools always smell of rubber?' It has a familiarity that's taking her way back into a past life. A life she doesn't want to remember.

With their footsteps echoing, they advance down the hallway.

A school cleaner calls out to them, 'Are you looking for the two little girls that are with Miss Foster?'

Luca, replies, 'Yes.'

The cleaner with her head down carries on sweeping, 'Second door on the right.'

Entering the classroom, they spot Miss Foster, who has the look of a woman who'd woken up one morning, to discover that her youth had passed her by before she'd had any fun. She has eyes of deep blue that would doubtless fix you in ice, should you dare disagree with her, or talk out of turn. Amalee and Darcy are perching on the edge of two red plastic chairs at the front of the classroom. Spotting him, they run and hug him, each holding a leg. Looking at Miss Foster, like a detective would, he asks, 'Do you know if Julia dropped them off this morning?'

Before Miss Foster can respond, Amalee, declares, 'Yes daddy, she did. Is mummy ok?'

'I'm sure she's fine, probably just fallen asleep, that's all.'

Smiling, Darcy remarks, 'Mummy sleeps all the time daddy.'

Walking back to the car, Luca tells the girls, 'Sam is going take you for a cake and milkshake, why I go to see mummy. Is that ok?'

Sam and the girls walk off towards Fulham Road, and Luca drives off in the opposite direction to Julia's flat.

Pulling up outside her flat, he sees the curtains still pulled. Entering the main entrance, he presses his index finger on the doorbell. With no answer, after a few more seconds, he pushes it again. Inserting the key that Julia gave him on his last visit, into the lock, he finds the door is already open.

It was strange for Julia to leave the door open. He'd always told her to lock it double whenever she was in. Pushing on the door, he calls out, 'Julia, are you in?'

There's no reply, just silence. Entering the hallway, a blast of air streams past him with it an aroma of polish. Seeing her bags on the floor, he calls out again 'Julia, are you there?'

Again, there's no answer. Noticing the door to the lounge ajar, he opens it gently. A faint smell of her perfume is lingering in the room. Scattered toys are on the floor, but otherwise, he sees nothing of concern. Going into her bedroom, he looks around, but it's empty. Now back in the lounge, he's about to close the door, when he spots the top end of her mobile phone on the floor, sticking out from the side of the sofa. Stooping to pick it up, he notices spots of blood on the carpet around the phone. Scanning the sofa and the surrounding areas, he sees dribbles of blood everywhere. A chill streaks through his veins, but he knows he can't stand there letting the numbness take him. His heart pounds and his head swirls, as he fumbles in his pocket for his mobile phone. Pressing Rick's number, he can't believe he's about to string the accompanying words together, 'Rick, Julia's gone missing; there's blood all over the place.'

Standing on the cracked pavement outside the flat, awaiting Rick's arrival, he paces back and forth like a caged lion, imagining her screams, begging for help. The clouds above him are dark, no rain has fallen, but the smell of it is in the air — a shock of white lightening forks silently across the grim sky. Two seconds later a crash of thunder cries out from the steel grey clouds as if

the heavens might split apart altogether.
Looking to the end of the road, towards Munster Road, he spots the blue flashing lights of Rick's car, that are little more than smudgy illuminations in the now torrential rain. Rick's car comes to a stop in front of the red-bricked apartment block. Exiting the vehicle saying something to Luca; his voice lost beneath the thunder rolling overhead. Entering the lounge again, dread creeps over Luca, anaesthetising his brain. Rick's eyes are showing concern, as he lays his hand on Luca's right shoulder. Rick's voice made your bones vibrate. When he spoke, everybody turned, whether they knew him or not. Rick leaves his hand on Luca's shoulder and speaks words of reassurance, with a soft voice. For Luca, it was more how he spoke the words than the actual words themselves.

CHAPTER
41

Julia's uncertain how long she's been unconscious for and doesn't have the slightest idea where she is. As she recovers her senses, she comprehends she's lying prostrate on a beaten-up dark brown leather couch, in a strange looking gloomy room. A single light bulb is shining above her, which is eerily incandescent, giving the room an eerie hue. Feeling a throbbing pain in her head, she's half blinded by flashing spots in her eyes. Craving darkness and stillness, nausea is overwhelming her. The pains are so violent around her skull; she feels it's about to split open at any second. Her first thoughts are, if there's any mercy left in this world, he will kill her quickly and cleanly. But she perceived; a more protracted death awaited her.

A jet black Victorian wall clock on the decaying wall opposite her is ticking like a bomb. Panicking, she struggles to breathe. An emotional cry for help forces itself up in her throat as teardrops stream down her cold face. Pushing herself up from the couch, the only other noise she can hear is the echoing of dripping water in the distance. Dressed in flat black shoes, jeans and a powder blue V-neck jumper, she places her feet onto the floor and attempts to stand. Stumbling forward, clutching a metal rail that's bolted to the wall, on her left-hand side, she goes in search of a toilet. Hearing a rumbling sound getting louder and louder, then dissolving into the distance, she presumes it's a tube train.

In a small room off the corridor, she discovers what's left of an ancient bathroom. Finding the toilet destroyed, pieces of it are dispersed across the dirty brown stained floor. Sheets of grubby newspaper, hang on a rusty nail on the pale green tiled wall. Back in the corridor, Julia hears a rustling in front of her and encounters a giant rat. Sensing an urge to panic, she stands rigid staring at it, eyeball to eyeball. At that moment, she craves to hear Luca's voice and longs for his strong protective arms around her.

Further down the hall, she finds two rooms opposite each other; they're both empty. The place is vast; as she wanders further down the dim corridor, there are at least twenty rooms on the ground floor alone. Hearing more rustling noises coming from all directions, it's telling her she's not alone. She can still hear the dripping water, but nothing else. In the peculiar environment of her surroundings, she's conjuring up terrible scenarios; her negative notions are coming in waves. In many of the rooms, she finds abandoned painting easels and brushes, adorning the dirty floors. It looks as though people had been painting there many decades ago. Spotting a door ahead of her slightly ajar, it's allowing a soft glow of golden light to meander, like a thin stream across the dark corridor. Her mind tells her not to move, but her body drags her there to the light,
like a moth to a fire. Every step she takes there's a loud shriek from the rotting floorboards below her. Entering the room, she finds broken furniture strewn across the floor: chairs and tables without legs, cabinets without doors. There are cobwebs everywhere, including the chandelier that's suspended from the yellowing cracked ceiling. The floors are of oak plank beneath the dust; the walls a mix of brick and broken plaster. A fire is crackling in the old Victorian tiled fireplace on the far side of the room.

Jumping when the floorboards unexpectedly creak

behind her; she turns and shudders, initially not so much with fear but shock. Her face sets like rigor mortis and her teeth lock tight together — fear, now consuming every cell in her body, filling her with terror. Her eyes are roaming the room for escape options. The man is standing still like a statue, glaring at her. Straining her vocal cords, she screams, hoping someone would hear her. Sobbing, she shakes like a leaf in a hurricane, sensing a warm stream of liquid coursing down her legs into her shoes.

His poisonous stare is painful and piercing as if it's tearing her head apart. Sweating her heart feels like it's about to rupture, as he steps towards her.

With rage filling her belly, she scowls at him, 'Who are you? What do you want?'

Grinning at her, he laughs, merely adding fuel to her wrath. She yells again. 'Do you think this is funny?'

Shooting her a venomous look, his evil dull eyes, ogle at her with disgust. Devoid of any warmth towards her, he tells her, 'You are a foolish girl. Aren't you?'

Fear finds her again, telling her legs to go weak, and her heart to ache. Julia's mother once told her, 'There's nothing to fear but fear itself.' But still, she couldn't silence its voice. She flinches when he turns and slams the door shut. Her brain converts to a mental soup of differing instructions, as he bears down on her. Standing motionless and emotionless, he gazes at her blonde hair and the most beautiful face he'd ever seen. Feeling his fingers crack, he flexes them in and out. Narrowing his eyes, sucking at the air, like it's become thick, he towers over her and without warning, punches her full in the face. Feeling the extensive force of the blow, she falls backwards, her head coming to rest on the wooden floor. Observing her laying the floor, her face sprouting blood, is giving him a sinister satisfaction. Grinning at her he's savouring the sting on his knuckles.

Looking up at him, stuck in a trance-like state, she watches his bloodshot eyes twitching under his bushy black eyebrows. The lines on his face are the imprinted story of a miserable life. It's as though his face belonged to another world — a face that wouldn't have looked out of place in a Victorian portrait.

She spots traces of blackened blood in his right nostril as he inclines his towering frame down over her. Putting his grubby hand out towards her face, she freezes solid.

Blood is covering her lips and bubbling from her nose as he grasps her by the back of her neck; she doesn't put up a struggle. To weak and disoriented, she gives in, as he leads her to a chair in the room's corner.

Sitting shaking on the bottle green wooden chair, she scratches her lips and face with her broken, dirty fingernails. Shuddering, she takes in deep breaths as he continues to stare at her. A bite of fear dances up and down her spine, as she thinks to herself 'I can't call this a nightmare, I'm awake?'

It reminds her of a reoccurring dream she's had since she was a teenager. The ordeal was invariably the same, tied up, naked and cold. A masked man with a long silver knife, making
sweeping actions, in front of her. He would get closer, then further away and then close again.

With her senses back, she roars at him, 'Tell me, what do you want, where are my girls?'

His croaky voice reverberates through her bones, and he casually tells her, 'All in good time, I need you to suffer first my love. I need to keep you here in hell, for a little longer.'

'I'm not in hell, you idiot. Hell's reserved for people like you. People, who know their actions are wrong, but do them regardless?'

Holding the syringe, the look in his angry eyes, confirms to Julia the outcome. She's going to die.

CHAPTER
42

After leaving Rick at the scene with the forensic team, Luca makes his way to see to Amalee and Darcy. Who are being looked after by Julia's friend Tina. In the early evening sunshine, he parks outside Tina's house in Finlay Street. Tina's peering out onto the street from her front window. Spotting Luca exiting his car, opening the front door, she meets him halfway down the small front garden path. Luca explains the situation out of earshot of the girls, and she invites him into the house.

Entering the house, Amalee rushes to him, clutching him by the arm, 'Is mummy sick again Daddy?'

'No, she's fine my love, where's Darcy?'

Tina interrupts, 'She's playing upstairs.'

Darcy comes bounding down the stairs, wearing the facial expression of a child unwrapping an enormous Christmas present, 'Daddy, Daddy.'

For Darcy happiness is simple. Its hugs with her Mum and Dad.

He tells the girls, 'You will need to stay with Tina for the night, and I will see you tomorrow.'

The girls know Tina and her two girls well, and it's not a problem for Amalee and Darcy. But it is for Luca, he hated telling them lies, and it's breaking his heart.

Driving back to Julia's flat, he phones Franco at the restaurant and tells him of the situation. Franco's reaction isn't good. He bawls at Luca, 'I know that prick Mason has something to do with this, I know it.'

'Calm down Franco. I don't need this. Let me deal with it. I'll call you later with any news. Can you let Martina know what's going on?'

The sun is disappearing over West London when he arrives back at the scene. He can see at least twenty police officers carrying out door-to-door enquiries. Standing in the early evening sun, he sees a small group of neighbours, gossiping on the opposite side of the road to Julia's flat.

Entering Julia's flat, both Sam and Rick look concerned. Luca knows from their faces and their body language something is wrong. Sam tells him, 'Forensics have found something, boss.'

She's about to tell him what, when one of the forensic team comes over and shows him a small transparent container. In the container are two pieces of a latex glove. The news hits Luca like a cluster bomb, exploding in his head. The harrowing scenes from the recent murders play over in his head, as though they are on a loop. Pacing back and forth; the pain is too much to cope with, too hard to deal with. No matter how hard he tries, his brain is unwilling to let the brutal images go.

Leaving the scene, he heads for the station with Sam and Rick. When they reach the car park, it's jammed to capacity. Rick chirps up, 'Looks like the governors called everyone in?'

Luca's governor, George Williams is waiting in reception for them, and they head to the top floor and congregate in George's office.

George tells Luca, 'I will give you all the support I can. I've brought everyone in, including those who have recently finished their shifts.'

He adds, 'We have checked all the hospitals in the area. We've also gathered all CCTV images surrounding Julia's flat.'

'Thanks guv, I feel I should be doing more, but I

understand we need to do it in the correct way.'

'Your right, I've also squared it with my governor to keep you involved in the case.'

Luca thanks him and leaves the room, feeling he needs a few minutes alone to find solace, and get his thoughts together.

Going through a list of places Julia could be, in his mind, ticking off mentally the ones he'd already checked. A gentle tap on the door brings him out of his thoughts, it's Rick, 'We're all here for you, boss.'

Luca, rubbing his eyes with the base of his palms, tells him 'I know Rick. I just needed a few minutes to get my head together, that's all.'

Rick sits down opposite Luca, 'Julia doesn't deserve this Rick. I lost her a year ago, I'm just getting her back, and now I may have lost her for good. And it's all down to this bloody job.'

Rick asks, 'Do you think this is down to Mason?'

'That's what Franco thinks, but I'm not sure if he's capable of it, or why he would want to do it.'

Rick adds 'Unless he's totally off his fucking rocker.'

'No, there's got to be more to it.'

'We will find her, boss, I know it.'

'We've got to Rick, not just for me but the girls. They haven't got a clue what's going on. I feel I need to be out there looking for her, but where do I start?' A sigh escapes his lips, 'It's killing me.'

CHAPTER
43

Awakening bleary-eyed and unshaven, Luca glances up at the clock, its 5.15 am. He's been asleep at his desk for twenty minutes. With every waking minute now intolerable, he's powerless to relax or concentrate on anything other than finding his beloved Julia. Sitting with his face in the palms of his hands, his adrenaline levels are rising through the roof — his inner dialogue whispering negative thoughts, like a machine gun blasting through his head. With his failures evident, he's finding his answers inadequate. Pictures of Julia are flooding his head, her face as pretty as the first day he met her. Her eyes were twinkling with laughter, her teeth gleaming. His mind is all over the place, unwilling to think anymore, he jumps to his feet and decides to take a walk to clear his head.

Squinting in the immediate brightness of the morning sun, he heads to Hyde Park. It may be a beautiful bright summer morning, but a never-ending dark cloud is consuming all around him. When he reaches the park, the sun is streaming through the trees, veiled in the daintiest of mists. The only noises he can hear are his footsteps and the early morning birdsong. Strolling along the gravel footpath, he reaches the Serpentine Bridge. Gazing out on to the lake, he takes a deep breath and closes his eyes. Placing his hands in front of his face, he breaks down in tears.

Walking through Knightsbridge on the way back to the station, his mind clears and he focusses on the day ahead. With bakeries and cafes opening for early trade, he can smell the delicious aromas, around him. A long line of black cabs is lining the road outside a large hotel. The cab drivers are chatting to each other by the entrance, undoubtedly waiting for early punters going to Heathrow Airport.

Arriving back at the station the car park is still full. Entering the station, Sam is standing at the front desk, Luca asks, 'Any news?'

With anguish in her eyes, Sam shakes her head. He tells her, 'Can you get the team together in the meeting room for 8 am?'

Luca's sitting at his desk mulling over plans for the day ahead, when Rick enters his office, like an out-of-control bulldozer, 'Boss, I've just taken a call, someone's discovered another body.'

Rick's words pass through Luca like a tornado. The despair he's feeling is all-consuming.

Luca bellows at Rick, 'Where?'

'Empty house in Orminston Grove, Shepherds Bush.'

'Is it Julia?'

'We don't know.'

Holding his palms to his ears trying to block out her screams, it doesn't work. They only grow louder. There is nothing left to feel, nothing left to say, nothing left but the void that's enveloped his mind in a swirling blackness. Grabbing the keys from the desk, he tells Rick 'Get Sam and meet me in the car park.'

Rick's sitting in the driving seat with Luca beside him, seconds later, Sam scrambles into the back. Gazing straight ahead Luca's in deep thought, not saying a word. Rick slams the black BMW into gear and roars away leaving smoke from the tyres, shrouding the station car park. Leaning forward, Luca plunges his finger on a button on the dashboard, sending blue lights and sirens blazing. He feels like a cow in a truck going to the slaughterhouse, only the cow doesn't know where it's going, but Luca does.

Nothing's said, even when Rick is hitting 60 mph, on the wrong side of Kensington High Street. Reaching Shepherds Bush, Rick turns into Orminston Grove, immediately spotting a police car parked up 100 yards in front with its lights flashing. Putting his foot down on the accelerator, stops the car, a yard short of a parked police car.

Ripping off his seat belt Luca's about to open the door when Rick puts his arm across and holds him back in his seat, 'Not in a million years boss, you're not going in there before us.'

Slamming his head back against the head restraint in frustration, he knows Rick is right. Sitting rigid his heart is pounding, as he waits to hear if it's Julia in the house.

The property is a red bricked two-story Victorian terraced house. Entering the hall, Rick and Sam are greeted by two officers, who leads them to the dining room at the rear of the property. The house is void of all furnishings and floor coverings. When they reach the doorway of the dining room, they stop in their tracks. The victim is a female with black hair and dark brown eyes. Her black leather skirt is up around her waist and her underwear removed. One leg is lying flat with the other one raised, her thighs parted. The girl's body is laying on the blue-tiled floor, looking like a ghoulish mannequin. Her face, graceful in life is grey, her eyes are open and her mouth slack. Tightened around her neck is a leather belt, but there are no other signs of injury.

Luca shouts from the hall, 'Is it Julia?'

Rick calls out, 'No boss, it's not.'

With feelings of joy and anguish, the hairs on the nape

of his neck are bristling. Luca's been skilful at camouflaging his broken insides for days, but his mask of pretence is crumbling fast.

Rick tells him, 'It's not the same MO as the others boss, someone's strangled her.'

When the doctor and forensic team arrive, the three of them leave and head for the car and Albert Mason's home address.

Pulling his Land Rover to a stop outside Albert's house, Franco exits the car like a greyhound out of trap one. The ornate black gates are open, and he sees Albert in the drive lifting a suitcase out of the boot of his Bentley. Striding across the drive, a burning rage is hissing through his body. With chest muscles bulging and biceps straining, he grabs Albert by the collar and pulls him over and onto his back. With an enormous thump, Albert's towering frame strikes the gravelled drive with force.

Straddling him Franco seizes him by the throat, holding his huge hairy right fist directly above Albert's face 'I didn't like you the first time I met you, now you've crossed the fucking line, now it's fucking war. Tell me where she is, or I won't stop until your smashed. I don't mean just smashed to pieces. I mean fucking dead.'

'What the fuck are you on about, you dumb bastard?'

'Where's Julia, that's what I'm on about?'

'Who the fuck is Julia?'

'You know who she is; you prick, tell me, where is she?'

Arriving at Albert's house, Luca and Rick see all hell breaking loose before their eyes. They hear Franco screaming at Albert, 'There isn't a place you can hide, I will destroy you. I don't care how it happens. I will eliminate anyone who attacks my family.'

Dragging Franco off, Rick leads him away towards the gates at the front of the house. Franco's knuckles are white from clenching his fists, his face red with rage. He tries to break free from Rick, but Rick holds him back and shoves him up against the wall that fronts the house. Albert gets up, brushing himself down, his nose a bloody mess. Luca notices an elderly grey-haired woman, looking out of the bottom right-hand window of the house.

Albert yells at Luca 'Your brother's a fucking maniac, what's he on about, who the fuck is Julia?'

Luca calmly tells him, 'We need to speak; let's go inside.'

Opening the front door, Albert guides him through to the lounge. Shaking, Albert pours himself a large scotch and asks, 'What the hell was all that about?'

'My brothers got it into his head; you know something about the disappearance of his sister-in-law, who is also my wife.'

'What, are you crazy, I don't know your wife, let alone have anything to do with taking her.'

'Where were you yesterday?'

'I was in Scotland, I've been there for two days. I've been on a business trip, plenty of people up there can vouch for me.'

Luca is taking details, when he sees Rick returning to the house, minus Franco.

Appearing in the lounge Rick tells Luca, 'I've calmed him down. He's gone back to the restaurant.'

'Thanks Rick, I'll talk to him later.'

After questioning Albert for another fifteen minutes, they leave the house.

Thirty minutes after Luca and Rick had left the house, Albert's in his study, when his mobile rings, 'Albert Mason.'

'What was going on outside your house earlier?'
'Who's this?'
'Who do you think it is?'
'Don't piss me about, who is it?'
'It's Jack of course, your brother.'

When Albert left Bagleys Lane School, his brother Jack's life became intolerable. He suffered dreadful bullying, the other kids making it their mission to make his life hell. They would insult, humiliate and attack him whenever they got the opportunity. Jack related it to being pursued daily by a pack of wolves. The bully's telling him many times; they wished he was dead like his father. When the bullying began, Jack's social anxiety worsened. Everything he did or said got slapped down, so he quit doing everything. He wouldn't get involved in any activities and didn't want to speak to anyone. Whenever the teacher left the classroom for a brief period, the other kids would gang up on him. Hitting him with pens, pencils, rulers and anything else they could get their hands on. On his way to and from school, there was never time to catch his breath. After his studies concluded, he would make his way to the toilet block in the playground and hide in one of the cubicles. He'd then wait until the school playground was clear of children, then sneak out, cutting across the deserted tarmacked playground and out into Bagleys Lane.

To get to his home there was no alternative route, so he would take his chances and run the gauntlet most afternoons. His heart would sink if he came upon a crowd of kids standing outside the local sweet shop, or on a street corner.

When he reached home, no one would be in so he'd go straight to his bedroom. When his mother or Albert came home, he'd act as though nothing had happened. As time went on, he got so depressed he avoided going to go to school whenever he could get away with it. Having no motivation, he didn't want to leave his bed. Feeling worthless to everyone, he told no one, so there was no protection or help. It wasn't merely the beatings for him; the mental bullying was worse. It's now damaged him beyond repair.

When Albert attended the same school, he'd beat anybody to a pulp if they upset him or Jack. He would then use his silver tongue, to get out of trouble with the teachers. Jack told Albert about one specific boy, who continually taunted him by telling him, his father killed himself because his sons were such losers. Albert, who at the time was attending St Henry's in Fulham Palace Road, met Jack at the school gate that afternoon. Jack pointed out the boy and Albert followed him. Albert confronted the boy in a side street and beat him up. Two days later the boys older brother approached Albert outside the off-licence in Bagleys Lane. There ensued a violent fight. Albert beat him so severely; they rushed the boy to the hospital where he remained for several days. Albert only received a caution from the police because the other boy had attacked him first. No one at the school ever bothered Jack again.

There were stages in Jack's life when daydreaming took over everything, which made him feel trapped in his mind. With no way to navigate out, he would withdraw into fantasy every waking hour. It was the first thing he needed to do when he woke up in the morning. In his later years, amid the bewildering, terrifying mix of diverse voices, there wasn't a day when he didn't imagine killing someone. He realised he had a lot of hate in his heart and was having internal fits of madness and mayhem daily. He could now hate people on a whole different level. There was something in his head that made him think it was appealing to kill. Aroused not by the violence and death; it was the build-up and the games before the slaughter, that furnished him with a massive surge of control and excitement.

CHAPTER
44

Luca and the team are assembling in the conference room for their 8 am briefing with their boss George Williams. With a determined stride George bounds into the room, his seven o'clock shadow already evident.

With no preamble, he proclaims, 'One course of raising awareness of a missing person, is using the media to publicise it. And as you know, we've held back on this for the last couple of weeks. But we now think it's time to put it out there to the public.'

Rick whispers to Sam, 'About fucking time.'

George looking up from his notes, 'Did you say something, Rick?'

Rick, smirking grunts, 'No boss.'

George continues, 'I am attending a press conference at 1 pm today, to appeal to the community for help in finding Julia. I will also ask for information regarding the murders of the three girls.'

He adds, 'We've drawn in an investigation team from Scotland Yard and two specialist search teams from other parts of London. I have designated another specialist team to interview all known associates of Julia. We have another team checking out her financial history and telephone activity, over the last couple of months. They will likewise look at her emails, internet and social media usage, which will assist us in finding her.'

He asks the team, 'Carry on concentrating on the places and locations, where we know Julia's closely associated with. Especially over the last three weeks. Also, carry on looking at all the CCTV you can find, and go beyond the areas we are already covering. We know she's visited the Chelsea and Westminster Hospital recently. We also know she met with Luca at Fulham Broadway and the Bluebird restaurant over the last two weeks. We are drawing on as many resources as we can to search areas, such as police dogs and a police helicopter. Volunteer search teams are also giving valuable help. As the standard, we will keep overall responsibility for the search. We've provided a coordinator to assist with the administration and control of the volunteer organisations. After my broadcast, we will have one of our officers here managing any potential sightings. I assure you, we will not leave any stone unturned until we get Julia back and find the killer of the recently murdered girls.'

George's words give Luca a renewed optimism, as he organises the team for the long day ahead.

CHAPTER
45

Opening her eyes, Julia feels something digging into her skin. Glancing down, she sees a cable binding her wrists to a metal pipe that's jutting out from the brick wall to the side of her. Looking around, she realises she's in a different room. To the right-hand side of her, on the dirty floor is a red flask and a packet of sandwiches from M&S. The daylight's dwindled, giving the room a look of an old photograph, making everything in the place a peculiar shade of grey. Tugging at the cable that's chafing her slender wrists, she leans her neck forward, biting at the cable, wriggling her hands-free without too much effort.

Rain is dripping through the cobwebs from cracks high in the roof above her. Rising to her feet, a repugnant odour of damp and rot fill her nose and throat. Approaching the door at the far end of the room, her footsteps echoing. Painted in a 1950s hospital green, the surface of the door is flat and shiny, like the front of a stainless-steel refrigerator. Trying to free the door with her bare hands is in vain. The door is staying firmly in its place. With no handle, lock or hinges, there's nothing to get a grip on to. Straining her ears for sounds, there's total silence. Scanning the spacious room, she sees twisted ivy has found its way through the ceilings and windows, tangling its tentacles like spidery fingers around the room. The building looks like someone had abandoned it, decades before she'd even been born.

Walking back to the other side of the room, she sits down next to the flask and sandwiches; her thoughts turning to Amalee and Darcy. Fumbling in her pocket for her credit card holder, she opens it and takes out a photograph of Luca and the girls, sitting on the grass eating ice creams on their recent visit to Bishops Park. Clutching the photo tight Julia smiles, visualising the wonderful times they'd had together. Staring at their faces, she bursts into tears.

She speculates, what the girls are going through, but deep down knows Luca will comfort them. Looking at the photo, she can see Amalee's blond hair blowing in the summer breeze. Her beautiful face turned towards the sun. Her feet, dancing like she can't tame them. She sees Darcy looking sweet and comical. For Darcy, happiness is simple; it's just cuddles.

She thinks to herself, 'What I would give now to hear their beautiful laughter, filling the air with delightful sounds.'

Being apart from Luca for a year had been tough enough. But meeting up with him over the last few weeks has brought back feelings she'd tried to hide deep within herself. No man had been the object of her desire in the previous twelve months. She had put love from her mind, discarding it as though it was an old dress she'd outgrown.

Her breath catches in her throat when she hears footsteps on the other side of the wall. As the door creaks open, he enters and slams the door shut behind him, sending the cobwebs above her head swinging in the breeze — the room's cast in flickering shadows, from the greasy candle he's carrying. With his face frozen in a gruesome pose, his lips are curling and his nostrils flaring. Feeling clammy, cold sweat is glistening on her forehead. Her eyes are wide as if someone's coming to deliver the fatal blow.

Shrieking at him at the top of her voice, 'Go away you

fucking psychopath, get away from me, piss off.'

The heavy air in the room is permeated with the scent of her body; her terrified eyes not lost on him. With excitement building in his chest, he shakes his head violently. Covering his mouth with his hand, hiding his decaying teeth. His thoughts will not dislodge, they're driving him on, making him the demon he is. Wanting to get rid of the hideous thoughts, he can't and won't. Confusing and inflaming him; they are his worst enemies, yet his dearest friends.
Slowly putting the latex gloves on, he runs his long spindly fingers over the gleaming steel knife he's carrying. Pressing his fingers to his lips, he raises his eyebrows, 'Are you nervous?'

Caught in a trance-like state, she stares at his eyes, which are now void of all emotion. When he speaks, it's slow, in a business-like tone, 'You say I'm a psychopath, I'm just wired; differently, that's all. Anyway, I don't care what you think of me, as long as you obey me.'

CHAPTER
46

After Jack's phone call, Albert's agreed to meet Jack near to where they lived as kids, in Bagleys Lane. Albert arrives at William Parnell Park, locally known as Pineapple Park at 8.15 pm. The laughter of children in the park had long since died, along with the sunlight. The twilight has stolen the colours of the day and the scene around him looks like an old black and white photograph. The park got its name because of an incident that happened many years ago. Legend says, a shipment of pineapples arrived at the docks and a local man stole a box. He then took it to nearby William Parnell House and distributed it to the families who lived there.

With his eyes drifting over to the massive graffiti strewn park wall. Albert's mind wanders back to the bleak wet February afternoon when his mother Florence told him about his dad's suicide. Again, he avoids thinking about what his father went through, and mentally holds up a hand to the thoughts, like a copper stopping traffic. When they were kids growing up in Bagleys Lane, he got on well with Jack and acted as Jack's protector and guardian from an early age.

Jack had just reached seventeen when a doctor committed him to a psychiatric hospital for a short period. After he returned home, whenever Albert asked him about it, Jack would clam up and change the subject. In those days, no one other than Albert seemed to give Jack the time of day, including their mother. Florence had always disapproved of him and would continuously nag at him to find more friends and stay out of the house. In their early twenties, for whatever reason,

Albert and Jack drifted apart. The last time Albert had heard from him was over fifteen years ago when Jack told him he was off to live in Scotland.

Looking down at his watch, it's 8.35 pm, Jack's late. Jumping, he feels a hand on his shoulder. In the fading light, the colossal figure of Jack is standing behind him.

Giving Albert a crooked smile, Albert laughs, 'You scared the shit out of me.'

'No one scares the shit out of you Albert. How are you?'

Albert puts out his arms, and they hug. Sitting down on the bench, Albert smiles at him, 'I've been sitting here reminiscing about the old days when we lived here with mum and dad. Do you remember the sweet old shop in Bagleys Lane that sold penny sweets? It's still there, but the sweets are not a penny anymore. Do you remember the school holidays, every day we would be out in the streets playing as if every drop of daylight were sacred?'

Not responding, Jack glares back at him with nothing in his eyes.

Albert carries on, 'They were good days, I remember the noise, laughter and the quarrelling in the streets. In the summer months, mothers, grandmothers and aunts would stand in the street chatting and laughing until late?'

Jacks eye's simmering with spite, 'I don't remember any good times Albert. Only bad times.'

With tears in his eyes he tells Albert, 'After you left school, the same boys would tease and assault me. When the other kids realised I was too afraid to fight back. They would join in. When the girls saw what the boys were doing, even they would push me around the classroom if the teachers weren't there. It was so bad I didn't feel safe, even with the teachers present. I remember crying on my walks home and crying in my bedroom when I got back from school. Hearing the kid's in my head, I slept with my head underneath the pillow. The voices would start as a whisper and slowly growing louder and louder. Sometimes the voices would wake me up in the middle of the night, and it would take me hours to fall back asleep.

'That's sad Jack. When I see your face, I only see good childhood memories.'

Jack tells him, 'I think of dad often and the way those scumbags treated him when he worked in the city. When we lost our dad, I was so devastated, I wanted to die and join him. We had no money and were always skint. I remember mum crying, clutching her purse and telling us; she'd had enough. Leaving the house, slamming the door behind her, times were so hard for her.'

With his voice now growing darker than a mausoleum, he adds, 'I want to protect you Albert as you protected me against the bullies who terrorised me all those years ago. At school, you were my big brother who slapped my bullies down, when the teachers did fuck all.'

'What are you on about Jack? I don't need protecting. I assure you I can look after myself.'

Jack yells, 'You don't understand, I know more people want to hurt you. Believe me, Albert, they want rid of you.'

His words are coming out like they're not coming from Jack himself. And when Albert tries to speak, Jack talks over him.

Rambling on, Jack tells him, 'I have strange thoughts and see things no one else does. Certain people in this world don't deserve to live and I can't let it go. You must know Albert; it's impossible not to hurt people from time to time.'

Albert snaps back 'What do you mean by that, what are you going on about?' Jack doesn't respond.

The tall, spindly figure of Reg, looking like something out of the Hobbit, is hiding nearby in the shadows of a large oak tree, listening intently to their conversation. He'd also heard the discussions at the restaurant between Luca and Franco, regarding Albert. He even knew Albert was behind the beating at his house.

Perched on the edge of the park bench, Jack's rocking back and forth. His eyes unblinking and his hair rustling in the summer night breeze.

Speaking with the fluidity of an ape with a migraine, he tells Albert, 'No matter how I try; I can never let it go. I have sought help, but no one listens. I now realise I have to put things right for you and dad.'

To describe Albert as narcissistic would be like stating that a ball is round. He looked down on the weak as if they were subhuman. And Jack, his brother or not is now getting on his nerves.

Trying to end their conversation, Albert asks, 'Jack, can I give you a lift back to Hammersmith?'

'No, I will find my way back. Don't worry.'

'It's no trouble. I can go that way home.'

Jack puts up his hand and shakes his head, 'I said I would find my way home, don't worry about it.'

Reg watches Albert and Jack exiting the park, via the Bagleys Lane entrance. He sees Albert hugging Jack and then crossing the road to his car.

Jack turns right, walking towards the bottom end of Bagleys Lane. Albert calls out, and points in the opposite direction, 'Jack, Hammersmith is that way.'

Jack does not look back or respond and carries on walking. As Albert pulls away, Reg exits the park entrance melting into the gloom. He follows Jack.

Jack's gait is uneven like his legs were different lengths. He wobbles as he walks, lurching from side to side. Every step looking as though he's about to stumble.

Reg watches as Jack turns right into Townmead Road. A street lamp flickers and Reg momentarily loses him but then sees the grim outline of his shadowy figure, crossing the road up ahead.

In the murky shadows, Jack senses someone's following him. His pulse quickens, looking for an escape route. Upping the pace, he walks faster and turns into a dark alley, and to the safety of its shadows. In the distance, sirens wail. From an open window, he can hear the voices of a man and a woman shouting at each other. A can rolls back and forth in the darkness and a scruffy cat appears, looks at him with unblinking green eyes, and stalks off.

Jack is thinking of the walk ahead of him when he's startled by a figure behind him in the gloom. A young woman grasps his arm, pulling him towards an open doorway. Her look of desperation stirs something inside him. Despite the temptation and a burning desire deep inside him, he shoves her aside and carries on walking. The girl is persistent and asks him for money and pointing to concrete steps leading to a boarded-up basement flat. Reaching the bottom of the steps, the basement's cluttered with fast food wrappers and trash. He lets out a small whimper as she pushes up against him and kisses his cheek, telling him, 'You smell fucking awful.'

The slight pressure of her thighs, provide him with a momentary surge of pleasure. Moving nothing but his eyes, his mind races, while every muscle stays rock still. Slivers of moonlight are shining down, igniting the grimy concrete floor. She's in her early forties, with shoulder-length chestnut hair. Looking up at him, smiling encouragement, her eyes widen. Without warning, he seizes her by the throat with one hand, ramming his other, into her face splitting her mouth. Screaming for help nothing comes out.

Plunging deeper and deeper within a sea filled with her mistakes. Getting to the bottom she knows, no one would save her. Closing her eyes, she forgets about the world, the world that's broken her. Bruised and battered, he leaves her alone with only the rats and insects for company.

Peering out from the steps into the dark street the wind's picked up, bringing with it dark clouds that hide the starry sky. The air smells of rain as he heads towards the river.

CHAPTER
47

Martina's busy preparing menus for the day ahead when Reg enters, 'Morning Reg.'

Without looking at her, he mumbles 'I saw Mason last night.'

'Where?'

'The park in Bagleys Lane, about 9 pm.'

'What the hell were you both doing in a park at that time of night?'

'Over the last few days, I've been following him whenever I can.'

Before Martina can inquire why he goes on, 'He met a man.'

'Do you know who the man was?'

'I didn't know him, but by the conversation they were having, I'm sure it was his brother.'

'Was there anyone else with them?'

'No, they were alone.'

'What were they were talking about?'

'Mason didn't say a lot. The other man did most of the talking. I could hear them chatting about the suicide of their father. The other man also talked about punishing people and wanting to protect Albert, as Albert had protected him when they were young. In the end, Mason seemed like he couldn't wait to get away.'

'How long are you here for?'

'Till midday, then I need to get to the V&A for my shift.'

'I'd appreciate it if you would talk to Luca, is that ok?'

Reg grunts, yes and heads for the backyard. Retrieving her mobile from the back pocket of her jeans, she phones

Luca.

Five minutes later, Franco comes breezing into the restaurant, Martina calls over to him, 'I need to talk to you.'

'Have they found Julia?'

'No, but Luca's on his way over.'

'What, with news of Julia?'

'No, I've just had an interesting conversation with Reg.'

Franco tells her, 'How the hell is Luca getting through all of this? If I stop to dwell on it, even a second, I get angry, I feel so bloody helpless. What must Luca be going through?'

Martina wipes a tear from her eye, 'I know what you mean, I can't concentrate on anything I'm
doing. I never knew missing someone could take over every fibre of your being.'
Franco adds, 'A big part of me worries if this family will ever be the same again.'
Sitting at his desk Luca's studying search reports with Rick when Sam comes hurtling into the room, 'We've got something boss.'

Continuing she tells them, 'Forensics have got some DNA from a piece of latex glove left at the scene. The even better news is, it's from a piece they found at Julia's flat. They're working on it now, to see if they can get a match.'

Stunned, Luca asks, 'How long will it take?'

'Normally, at least a week but they've told me they would pull out all stops, so hopefully today or tomorrow.'

Luca is about to respond when his mobile springs into action, it's Martina. She tells him about her conversation with Reg. Luca informs her he will be there in twenty minutes.

'Come on Rick. We need to get to the restaurant, get the car.'

'Sam, can you let me know as soon as you hear anything on the DNA result?'

'I am going over there now to see if I can rush matters along.'

Rick's sitting in the car with the engine running when Luca scrambles into the front seat. 'Step on it, Rick. Martina's just told me, Reg followed Mason last night to a park in Bagleys Lane. He met someone there, and he's sure it was his brother. He also heard most of their conversation. It turns out his brother wants to protect Albert. Reg also heard the brother mention my name, along with Flynn and Lane's in their conversation.'

Driving to the restaurant the sun is receiving the day as if everything was fine, and it's just another ordinary morning. Ordinary except his Julia is still missing. Luca's heart's ingrained with remorse, and his guilt is gnawing like a worm at the core of a rotten apple. A never-ending dark void is devouring everything, leaving him empty. He continues taunting himself, but no amount of analysis could turn back the clock. He had to get on with it and find her.

The restaurant's empty when Luca and Rick enter. Martina greets Luca with a hug, and he asks, 'Where's Reg?'

'He's in the back. I'll get him. There's no one upstairs at the moment, why don't you talk to him up there? I'll send him up.'

Two minutes later Reg appears at the top of the stairs. 'Hi Reg, glad to see you are on the mend, how are you?'

'I'm ok now thanks, most of the injuries were superficial.'

Getting to the point, Luca asks, 'Tell me exactly what

you saw and heard last night in the park.'

Reg tells him everything he heard and how he followed the other man when he left Albert.'

'Do you think he knew you were following him?'

'Not at first, but I think he noticed when we were in Townmead Road.'

'Where did you lose him?'

'He disappeared down a side street off Townmead Road, near to Wandsworth Bridge.'

'Was the man's name mentioned in their conversation?'

'Martina asked me that and I wasn't sure. But I think it may have been Jack.'

Rick takes a full description and statement, and both thank Reg.

When Luca gets to the bottom of the stairs, he phones Sam and asks her to check if Albert is at his office in Covent Garden. Two minutes later she calls him back and confirms he is.

Driving through Knightsbridge, Rick asks Luca, 'How the hell are you coping with this nightmare, boss?'

He tells Rick, 'Throughout my life; I've encountered and witnessed the traumas of death, loss and suffering. I have heard the heart-breaking tales of others who have suffered and experienced unspeakable horrors. But I have never felt like this. At the moment, there's no past or future. I'm just living by the moment. It's indescribable.'

'How are the girls coping?'

'To be honest Rick, I've not told them a thing. There's no point at the moment. They think she's not well, and that's it. Martina told me earlier she will take some time off from the restaurant, and look after them at her flat until we get news.'

Rick muses, 'Are you thinking what I'm thinking about

this brother of Albert's?'

'I am Rick. There's got to be a connection, between him, the girls and Julia. I think it's our only hope if I'm honest.'

Entering the car park of Albert's office, they spot his Bentley parked in his nominated spot, by the main entrance of the building. They're walking over to the entrance when Albert comes bounding out of the building. Ranting at them, 'What the fuck are you two doing here again, what's going on, this is harassment?'

Rick smiles, 'We've been missing you, Albert.'

Albert's face is priceless, a combo of dread and embarrassment. His eyes are twitching, 'Well, what do you want?'

'Calm down Albert.' Says Luca.

Luca's comment inflames him even more 'How can you expect me to calm down when you think it's ok to come to my company like the fucking Gestapo and make accusations about me.'

Rick barks, 'We've not made any accusations, yet.'

Albert's about to speak again when Luca holds up his hand, stopping him from wasting any more of his breath, 'We need to speak to you; we can do it in your office or at our place. You choose.'

The three of them enter the building and Albert shows them to a small room, off the reception area. The room is sparse and square with four red plastic chairs, a table and an empty water dispenser in the corner. Luca and Rick sit, but Albert stays standing.

Luca asks, 'Where were you last night between 8 and 10 pm?'

'Why are you asking?'

Rick growls, 'Just answer the question, Albert.'

Rick getting straight to the point asks, 'Tell us about

the man you met in the park last night, the park in Bagleys Lane?'

Albert asks, 'What the fuck. Have you been following me?'

Luca ignores his comment, 'Well.'

'If you must know I met my brother there.'

Rick asks, 'What did you talk about?'

Albert shakes his head, 'Just family things, that's all.'

Luca asks, 'What family things?'

Rick butts in, 'What's your brother's name?'

'His names, Jack, what is this, twenty fucking questions?'

Rick asks, 'Why the park?'

'Why not the park? He asked me to meet him there; that's why.'

'What other things did you talk about?'

'What has this got to do with you?'

Rick tells him, 'Just answer the question.'

'If you want to know, we were reminiscing about old times, when we were kids in the area, and that's it.'

Rick grins, 'That's touching Albert.'

Luca interjects, 'Before last night when was the last time you had contact with him?'

Fidgeting in the chair and smoothing back his hair, 'About fifteen years ago.'

'Why so long, did you have a falling out?'

'No, we didn't, he went to live in Scotland and we lost contact.'

'So, why's he back now?'

Albert crosses his arms, 'I am done talking. If you want anymore, I want my solicitor here. I'm not saying another word.'

Rick ignores him, 'Just one more thing, where's Jack living?'

'I don't know, he told me Hammersmith, that's all I know.'

Albert raises his right hand and looks Luca in the eyes, 'I want to end this, now.'

Slamming both his hands down hard on the table, Rick stands. With his bulk standing in front of Albert, he shouts, 'So why the fuck was Jack talking to you about revenge, on certain people, including DI Luca Rossi and Bryan Flynn?'

Albert's about to answer, when the receptionist opens the door and asks, 'Is everything ok Mr Mason?'

Albert puts up a hand, 'Yes, there's not a problem Karen, I'm fine.'

When she shuts the door, Albert seems to have calmed down, 'Look let's all sit down.'

Luca and Rick follow his instruction and sit opposite him. 'You need to understand that Jack has had problems all of his life. From an early age, he was relentlessly bullied. I knew he'd been in and out of mental institutions in his late teens. We lost touch when he reached his early twenties. By the state of him and how he was rambling on last night, he's probably been in and out of them most of his life. As I said, the last time I spoke with him was around fifteen years ago, when he phoned and told me he was going to move to Scotland.'

Luca, opening his hands asks, 'So what's this talk about revenge, on me, Flynn, Thomas and Robert Lane?'

'Last night I didn't have a clue what he was going on about. I don't know how your name and the other names came into it. I've discussed none of you with him?'

Rick asks, 'So we have three murdered girls, who fathers have had dealings with you and the boss's wife's gone missing. And you've never told him a thing?'

'I swear, I've not spoken to him for over fifteen years. I

don't know how he came up with those names. It shocked me.'

Luca leaves it there and tells Albert, 'If he gets in contact or you see him, I want you to contact me without delay. I mean it Albert, or your feet won't touch the fucking ground. Police business or not I will destroy you.

CHAPTER
48

Jack's eyes readjust in the gloom, the woman sleeping beside him is snoring, her mouth open. Saggy and past her prime, she's all bleached blond hair and dark roots. Having not slept for three days, he'd figured her company might do him good.

Prodding her in the face, he shouts at her, 'Come on, get up.'

There's no response. Shoving her in the ribs, she snorts and groans.

When he turns on the light, the woman's eyes flutter open, asking, 'Do you want some more?'

Exploding he shouts at her, 'I said, get up and get out, you bitch.'

The stench of unwashed clothes and the sour smell of old age is making the woman's stomach churn. She's a professional. He didn't have to tell her twice.
Crawling out of the squalid bed, he watches her dressing. Her breasts, reminding him of sacks of potatoes. Having already received her money she didn't speak. After squeezing into her tight denim jeans, she puts on her sweater and steps into her heels. Hearing blood rushing through his head, he grabs her wrist, ramming his free fist into her nose, spreading it across her face. Collapsing to the floor, holding herself in a fetal position, fear's consuming her. Gasping, she forces herself to her feet. The pounding of her heart, is invading her ears as she heads for the door.
In the forefront of his mind, Jack's focus is to single handily rid the world of the scum that hurt him and his family. He'd always known he had wickedness in him

and knew it would come out someday.

When detained in a mental hospital for the first time at age seventeen. He remembers thinking how ironic, even tragic, that the environment that had been created to help him was one of alienation, confusion, and helplessness - the qualities that exacerbated his vulnerability in the first place. When he arrived at the hospital for the first time, he was strip searched and put under constant surveillance. No rooms were available on his first night, so he had the pleasure of hearing the attendants talking all night, their conversations consisting of mainly cruel jokes aimed at the patients.

The next morning, he attempted to be friendly with the woman who was dispensing pills. Snarling at him, she told him, 'I can tell you, this one will suck the life out of you.' Handing him his pill, she laughs and calls for next in line.

Jack was never warned that his freedom would be curtailed, and could not leave the hospital. This made him think he was being punished for being ill.

Confined many times over the years under the Mental Health Act, suffering from schizophrenia.

His memories of Ward Two of the Glasgow Mental Asylum, are his worse. It was an 'acute admissions' ward, meant for people in a profoundly disturbing state, requiring plenty of care (and drugs). Detained on many occasions, he received forcible injections which left him traumatised. He also took part in assembly-line shock therapies, dished out by brutal nurses. He recalls the nurses behind their screens, observing the patients on the monitors. Cameras were also in the bathrooms and bedrooms. On one occasion, he heard screaming and shouting coming from the main corridor. A nurse had discovered a patient who had hung himself with a bedsheet. He was naked with cuts all over his body and blood was everywhere. Barely conscious he was pleading with the nurses to let him die, stating his life was over and he didn't want to live anymore.

Jack heard voices in his head and suffered from severe paranoid delusions. One of his habits was to abuse and accuse the staff and other patients. He would walk around the ward shouting at the top of his voice, 'You're not a nurse, and I'm not a patient. You're the fucking nut cases in here.'

Jack's never been a calm person. You'd never see him reading a book or watching a film. He demanded to be in the open. Even when let out to exercise, all he would do, was wander around the perimeter fence looking for a way out. In the asylum, time is marked by the coming and going of meals and medications. Every minute was purgatory for Jack. Most days the suffocation made his lungs feel like they were caving in. Feeling trapped and incarcerated in his mind. The mysterious voices in his head were adding new dangerous ideas all the time. Seeding a new identity and muddling up the rest. After dressing, he heads to the door. He needs to contact Luca Rossi and lay the trap.

CHAPTER
49

The noisy clamouring of the alarm clock jars Luca out of his restless slumber. Reaching out, he slams the off button as hard as he can. Jolting upright, soaked in sweat he realises, he's fully dressed. Feeling exhausted, virtually to the point he can't stand, he feels his mobile phone vibrating in his trouser pocket.

'What have you got Sam?'

'We've got a match boss. The results are on the way over.'

After a change of clothing and a shower, he gulps down the rest of his triple expresso. Double locking the front door behind him, he heads for the car. Sitting still in the car trying to calm himself, his knuckles are white as he lowers his head towards the steering wheel. Breathing hard, he sits up then slams his forehead against it, in frustration. Sweat is gluing his shirt to his back as the murders play over and over in his head. After all his years in the force, after all he had seen and wished he hadn't seen. The latest murders, the heinous deeds he had been witness to, are constantly coming at him. Driving along Brompton Road on the way to the station, he's reflecting on his visit to Tina's to see Amalee and Darcy. He gazes straight ahead, only half-aware of a world outside the claustrophobic comfort of his car. The road is an endless river of tarmac, baked under the brutal relentless sun. The pavements are moving like a great river of humanity. His senses are on high alert, and every colour is sharper, every noise louder. His mind drifts back to when he left the girls at Tina's. Standing with Tina at the front door saying their goodbyes to him, he remembers glancing from one to the other. Their brows wrinkling and both bursting into tears simultaneously. It shatters his heart that his girls are worried and want to know where their mum is and if she's ok. He'd never felt so guilty in his life, lying to them telling them everything would be fine and not worry. He searches deep into his mind, what he will say to them if Julia doesn't come back. He wonders to himself how he will ever explain that to them?

The mood is sombre when he arrives at the station. Murder cases are always hard on everyone. But when the wife of a DI goes missing, and it's linked to multiple horrific murders, it can't get much worse.

Rick and Sam are waiting for him in his office. Luca asks 'Have we got a name yet?'

Sam says, 'Should be any minute now. Did you get any sleep last night?'

Luca's about to respond when the phone on his desk rings. He looks at Sam and nods, 'You take it.'

Sam picks up the phone and looks up at Luca, 'It's the front desk, they've got someone on the phone, who wants to talk to you.'

Luca's shocked when the desk sergeant tells him, 'It's his next-door neighbour.'

The neighbour tells him he'd found Luca's front door wide open. Luca tells him he will be there as soon as possible and asks him not to enter the property. The neighbour agrees to stay outside until Luca gets there.

'You stay here Sam. I need to get back home. Get the car Rick.'

'Let us know as soon as a result comes through.'

Sitting next to Rick in the car, Luca tells him, 'I've got a bad feeling about this, I know I double locked the door.'

Putting on the flashing lights, they head to Parsons Green Lane.

Rick asks, 'What's this neighbour like?'

'To be fair, I've not had much to do with him since I moved in. He's got the sort of face you'd forget, even while you're looking at it.' Rick smiles.

Reaching Luca's house, the neighbour is standing in the shade by the gate.

After thanking the neighbour, they both enter the house. Straightaway Luca has a hunch something is wrong. A thin shaft of light cuts across the ceiling on the landing, and a rush of fresh air greets him. Though the day was one of the hottest days of the summer, he shivers as he crosses the threshold into the hall.

He tells Rick, 'Have a look around downstairs. I'll have a look upstairs.'

Reaching the top of the landing, he notices the bedroom door is ajar. He knew he'd shut it, as he always did. Entering the room, he detects an obnoxious odour and knows someone's been in the room. Adrenaline is coursing through his veins as he looks around the room, studying the scene. He's about to enter the en-suite when he notices a piece of white card folded on his pillow. Unfolding it, he scans the bold red writing, 'I warned you. Your pain is about to get a lot worse. Look under your pillow.'

His heart almost stops when he finds two-small photographs, one of Carol Lane covered in blood at her murder scene. The other is a blood-stained picture of Luca, Julia and the two girls sitting on the grass, eating ice creams in Bishops Park. His knees go weak as if his bones have no strength and his muscles are out of power. His brain firing out negative thoughts like a machine gun. The arguments in his head are getting so fast and disturbing; his mind is trying to shut down his body.

From the landing, he calls out to Rick, 'Rick, get up here quick.'

Rick responds, 'Is everything ok boss?'

'No, it's not, have a look at this.'

Descending the stairs, Rick's phone rings, 'Hi Sam, any news?'

'We've got a match.'

Rick looks up and nods at Luca, 'Who is it?'

'Jack Mason.'

CHAPTER
50

Sitting alone in the dark, dank room, gripping the homemade knife she's made. Julia's emotions are whirling like ocean currents, deep and strong. The knife is nothing more than a rusted piece of jagged metal, bound with some wire, she'd found amongst the rubble on the floor.
Hearing the groaning of the ancient floorboards, she realises he's about to return. Clutching the knife, she crawls across the filthy floor, hiding between the sturdy legs of an old wooden desk. Hearing the lock turn, she forces herself to take long forced breaths. Her eyes crack wide open, and her heart pounds as the door squeals open. Stepping from the shadows into the dim room. His figure is tall and hunched beneath his long drab coat that's as black as night. Observing him scanning the room, she hears his voice, which is low and throaty, 'I know you're here, I've been watching you. Are you under the desk?'

Panicking, she feels clammy; her face glistening with cold sweat. A multitude of goosebumps coating her skin. A sudden bright glare lights the room as he strikes a match, placing the flame onto the top of a candle he's holding. Putting the lighted candle on a shelf to the side of him, he advances on her. Dragging her to her feet from under the desk, he slaps her hard across her face. With blood running from the corner of her mouth, her trembling left hand reaches to wipe it from her face. Holding her right hand firmly around the knife, down by her side, acting composed, she says nothing. Shoving her in the back; he pushes her towards the middle of the gloomy room.

Trembling, she pivots and launches a frenzied attack on him, yelling and stabbing at him with the rusted knife. Kicking out at her, he catches her in the pit of her stomach, sending her reeling across the floor. Getting to her feet, the feeling in her legs have gone, and she skids to the floor. Looking up at him she sees blood on his face, but nowhere else. Sensing pain and wetness on her right hand, she glances down seeing the knife has bent inwards on itself, piercing her hand.

Bending down, he takes her by the scruff of the neck with one hand and punches her full in the face with the other. Falling to her knees, she begs him to stop, but it only fuels his violence. As the blows continue to rain down on her, she falls face down into the dirt.

Standing above her he thunders like a Vicar giving a sermon, 'I believe it's my right to rid you and other scum from this world. I don't want you to have things; they denied my father. I want you to suffer as he did. I want you and your family to know what pain and suffering feel like. Just like I did when my father killed himself.'

Feeling like someone had raked her over with a blowtorch, she opens her mouth to speak, but he continues his sermon, 'Do you know what else I want? I want to stop the scum from hurting
and pursuing my brother and believe me. I will succeed.'

Kicking out at her once more, he leaves the room. Trying to sit up her head crashes back to the dusty floor. Blood is covering her face and drying like plaster. Her legs shake as she eventually rises to her feet, her face raw with tears. Dazed, she sits back down on the floor and pulls a piece of dirty blue plastic sheet, that's laying nearby, over her. Memories and emotions surge in her head like a storm. Cold, lonely and in pain, she misses

Luca's arms around her and the warm kind-heartedness of her daughters.

CHAPTER 51

After phoning Albert, Luca and Rick had agreed to meet him at his wife's address, in Chelsea Harbour. Passing Chelsea Town Hall on their left Rick tells Luca, 'I don't know how you've got through the last few days. You must be in bits?'

'It's simple Rick, I love her so much and I can't let my daughters lose their mum. Coping with the loss of someone you love has got to be one of life's biggest challenges. I've experienced nothing like it. The pain is overwhelming. I'm experiencing all kinds of difficult and unexpected emotions, I never thought possible, from shock, anger, guilt to profound sadness. Over the last few days, I've doubted the stability of my mental health.'

With the red bricked towering chimney stacks of Lots Road Power Station in the distance, they pass the World's End Pub. Turning left into Lots Road, they head to Chelsea Harbour at the bottom of the road. As they pull into the parking area, Luca's phone rings, it's Sam. 'Boss, I've got plenty of info on Jack Mason. It's not good; he's been in and out of mental institutions since his teens. And it doesn't make good reading.'

'Thanks Sam, we've just arrived at Chelsea Harbour to have another chat with Albert Mason. Can you go through the reports, to see if it can provide any clues on Jack Mason's whereabouts?'

Exiting the car, the heat is stifling. A brief smile shows on Luca's face when Rick tells him, 'I'm sweating like a dog in a Korean restaurant.'

Entering the luxury apartment block, they approach the concierge who has a face as blank as a catalogue model. Rick declares, 'We're here to see Albert Mason.'

Calling the penthouse suite, she points them to the lift on the left-hand side of the reception area. When they exit the lift, Albert's standing at the door waiting for them, his face puffy — nursing a large whisky.

Looking out over the Thames through the massive panoramic window, Rick asks, 'I thought you lived in Notting Hill Gate Albert?'

'I do, my wife lives here, not that's it is any of your business.'

In the sunlight, Luca spots a thin scar crossing Albert's right cheek. He guesses from his misspent youth on the streets. Luca asks, 'Have you heard anymore from Jack?'

'I told you, I would let you know if I did.'

Luca asks, 'We urgently need to talk to him.'

Albert, sighs rolling his eyes, 'I haven't seen him, so I can't tell you anything.'

'You told us he was living in Hammersmith; he must have mentioned something else?'

Albert curls his long fingers into a clawed fist, using his hands to stress his words, 'Look, the last time I saw him he was walking down Bagleys Lane towards the river, that's it. There's nothing else.'

Rick butts in, 'I'm no London cab driver, but that's the opposite way to Hammersmith.'

Albert smirks, 'Perhaps he was off to feed the ducks on the river, how do I know?'

At that point, Rick feels like belting him straight between the eyes.

'I'm not sure what my brother is involved in, but when I met him in the park, he shocked me. The man's barking mad. I want nothing to do with him.'

Luca feels they are squandering time speaking to him and they leave. On the way down to the reception, he tells Rick, 'When I spoke to Reg he told me the same, he turned right instead of left. Reg followed him to Townmead Road but then lost him.'

Rick replies, 'Did you know a woman was assaulted, in a side street off Townmead Road on the same night?'

'No, I didn't. What happened?'

'Sam told me they think she was an addict on the game. Someone assaulted her and left her at the bottom of some steps that led to a basement flat. She's in intensive care in the Chelsea and Westminster Hospital.'

'Phone Sam and tell her to get down there and try to get information from the woman. Also ask her to get any CCTV checked out, around the areas concerned.'

He then tells Rick, 'Drop me off at Parsons Green Lane so I can pick up my car. I want to have another chat with Reg at the restaurant. I'll meet you back at the station later.'

After picking his car up, passing Chelsea Football Ground he phones Martina at the restaurant, 'Hi Martina it's me, I'm on my way to the restaurant. Is Reg still there?'

'Yes, he's just arrived. Do you have any news?'

'I think we are getting close. I'll tell you more when I get there.'

On entering the restaurant, Luca's met by Marie who hugs him like a lost love, with tears in her eyes, 'She's in the back boss.'

'Thanks Marie.'

Luca finds her in the kitchen talking to Reg, 'Could we have a chat Reg?'

Reg nods.

'Is anyone upstairs sis?'

'No, it's all clear.'

When they get to the top of the stairs Luca asks Reg to

sit down, 'Can I ask you a few more questions about the meeting between Albert and his brother Jack that you witnessed?'

'But I've told you everything.'

'Can you go over it again, particularly their conversation?'

'It was Albert who did most of the talking at first. He talked about when they were kids in the area. But I got the impression the other man was not interested. I remember him telling Albert; he didn't have any good memories, just bad ones.'

'Anything else?'

'The other man got agitated, and he talked about his bullying at school and how Albert protected him. He then rambled on about how he wanted to protect Albert now. He also talked about his father's suicide and how it hurt him.'

'Did he say why he wanted to protect Albert?'

'He told Albert, he knew certain people wanted to hurt him.'

'What was Albert's reaction to that?'

'Albert laughed and told him he didn't need looking after, and he could protect himself.'

'Did he say how he knew these people were going to hurt Albert?'

'No, not directly, he said he heard voices in his head. He also told Albert he'd been watching his career in the business world.'

'So, when you left the park, what happened?'

'I heard Albert offer him a lift home to Hammersmith, but the other man refused, saying he would make his way there. He walked towards the bottom of Bagleys Lane, which as you know is in the opposite direction to Hammersmith.'

Reg adds, 'I followed him, but lost him towards the end of Townmead Road, near Wandsworth Bridge. I turned right into Wandsworth Bridge Road and made my way home.'

'Is there anything else he said to Albert that might be of significance?'

'No, not really but Albert did tell him he smelt like a brewery, that's all.'

'Thanks Reg, you have been helpful.'

After updating Martina and Franco, Luca leaves the restaurant and heads back to the station.

CHAPTER
52

It's 9.30 pm, and Luca's working by the light of the green banker's lamp, on his desk. Staring at a line of photographs, spread out in a timeline, he's confident they're onto something. All along he'd toyed with the idea; the murders were about power; his opinion has now changed. He now thinks it's about revenge. Sam had told him earlier that evening; the woman attacked in the Townmead Road area had not regained consciousness and was still in a coma, in the Chelsea and Westminster Hospital.

Sam enters Luca's office, 'Have a look at this boss.'

Moving the photos to one side, Sam places a laptop on the desk. Pressing the start button, a film from a CCTV camera plays. The scene's misty. Sam points at the screen and a tall dark figure of a man, dressed in dark clothing comes into view. His pace is quick and he's walking with a limp.

'Where is this Sam?'

'Townmead Road, towards the end near Wandsworth Bridge Road. The good news is the timeline fits with his meeting with Albert and the woman attacked in the side street.'

She adds, pointing, 'This is where we lose him when he enters the alley. We have searched all other CCTV in the surrounding area but there's nothing else.'

'Can we get a closer look at his face?'

'We are working on it but it doesn't look good.'

'Great work Sam.'

'We will get her back boss.'

Luca smiles at her, 'I know Sam, thanks.'

Alone in his office rearranging the photos on his desk his mobile rings, 'Hello, Luca Rossi speaking.'

'Carefully listen to me. Meet me outside Barton House in Wandsworth Bridge Road at 11 pm. I will call you when you arrive. Believe me when I say, if you tell a single sole of our meet or I spot anything suspicious. She will die a painful death. I will then send parts of her to you and your fucking kids.'

Whoever is on the other end, then hangs up. Luca looks up to the clock; it's 9.55 pm.

Bursting through the back door of the station, into the car park, he heads for his car. Sitting in the car his knuckles are white with tension. Gripping the steering wheel with both hands, he deliberates on the task ahead of him.

Driving through the streets of West London, every hair on his head is standing to attention and every skin cell is tingling. Parking up in Wandsworth Bridge Road, he looks behind him, his fingers drumming on the steering wheel. His eyes dart along the road towards Barton House. Taking a deep breath, he makes a sharp U-turn and drives slowly, looking into shadows. Up ahead the road is busy with people standing outside bars and restaurants. He sees a man in a dark overcoat exit a pub. The man glares at him and shouts, 'Who are you looking at, lost your fucking boyfriend?'

Pulling the car against the curb, he turns off the headlights. The man who shouted at him, steps out into the road, hailing down a black cab. He sees another man of medium height and build, wearing a grey hooded sweatshirt, fleeing down a nearby alley. A handful of people are drifting from the bar, crossing the road, heading towards Wandsworth Bridge.

At 10.55 pm, the driver's door gives a squeaky yawn as Luca leaves the car. Stepping around broken beer bottles and a wet Tesco plastic bag, he walks along to Barton House. The tower block emerges on Luca's left-hand side, looking like it's standing on white stilts, pointing towards the sky, like a brick-built rocket. Turning left into Stephendale Road, he waits outside the main entrance.

At 11.01 pm his phone rings, inhaling, he puts the phone to his ear and answers, 'Luca Rossi, speaking.'

The gruff voice at the other end tells him, 'Listen to me carefully, leave your car where it is and cross Wandsworth Bridge Road. Walk towards Wandsworth Bridge and wait on the corner of Carnwarth Road.' The man then hangs up.

Reaching Carnwath Road, he waits on the corner. Two minutes later his phone rings again, and he answers, 'Now walk up Carnwath Road. About halfway up you will find a boarded off derelict building site, on the left-hand side. Enter from the right-hand side and go to the end of the path towards the river. You can enter the site through a gap in the wire fence.' Again, he hangs up.

Reaching the site, he can hardly see a thing in the dark pall of the night. Arriving at the gap in the fence there's a brief break in the clouds. And the soft, delicate light of a quarter moon lights up the sky.

Climbing through the wire fence his heart feels like a fist pounding the inside of his chest. Once through the fence, he comes upon the ruins of what must have been workers' houses — encroaching upon the road to his right. Straight ahead of him are massive old rusty green gates. His phone rings again, stopping him in his tracks. Answering, the chilling voice tells him, 'Come through the green gates and walk straight ahead, the gates are not locked.'

Once through the gates, continuing east, the surroundings become more abandoned and desolate, as he gets further into the site. The moonlight is picking out a potholed street, revealing the original brick road beneath. The warehouses that front the river are as black as Newgate's knocker, few of them owning windows. Luca's only a mile from his house in Parsons Green, but it seems he's entered another world. Coming to a small dirt street that's winding its way between two imposing buildings a hundred yards in front of him. He spots a tall figure of a man, in front of the larger of the two buildings. He takes a step forward and sees the man limping into the enormous dark building. Luca's heart beats fast as he sprints over to the building.
Stopping at the entrance, he hears a rope clanking on a flagpole, on the roof above him. As he
enters his torch is making elongated shadows, dance upon the walls, of the once magnificent Art Deco reception area — giving it an eerie atmosphere. He lets out a breath he doesn't even know he's holding, he spots a giant black rat on the floor to his right, staring at him with its beady black eyes.
The temperature drops as he enters further into the bowels of the extensive building, delivering chills down his spine. Ambling down the unnerving dark hallway, he hears the tapping sound of a branch against a window to his right-hand side. The abandoned building looks like it's been a drug den and homeless shelter for many decades. It's once beautifully tiled walls, now covered with graffiti and excrement, the floors littered with hypodermic needles, broken bottles and sewage. Horrible thoughts are bouncing around in his head, like the balls in a bingo machine. He freezes when from behind he

hears footsteps and a sinister laugh. Spinning around, he can't see anybody. Unexpectedly, there's a small popping noise, and he feels a sharp sting in the side of his neck. With a dazed expression on his face, he stumbles forward and crashes down to the floor, like a lead mannequin, out cold.

Waking from the drug-induced coma, Luca finds the room in darkness. Breathing in the stale air, he realises he's lying face-down with his hands and feet tied. A constant dripping noise is coming from the left-hand side, underneath is the echoing sound of footsteps that are getting louder and louder. Struggling to stand, to see what or who was coming, the rope binding his wrists and ankles pull tight — keeping him on the floor. In the shadowy gloom, he sees a tall silhouetted figure approaching. As the figure gets closer, Luca knows he's in trouble.

Rubbing his face, the man speaks like an auctioneer on speed, telling Luca, 'Welcome to my world, DI Rossi. I've waited weeks for your visit and I can't wait to get started.'

Boiling with fury, Luca grinds his teeth, clenching his jaw so tight it hurts. In a fiery burst he snarls, 'I know who you are, Mason, you won't get away with this, I promise you.'

Luca's sudden outburst poses no threat to Jack, who continues to play the role of a ghostly freak, keeping his facade of dread and mystery. Jack closes his eyes and summons a deep breath. Holding it in, he looks up to the yellowing ceiling, 'DI Rossi, you have no control here, so keep your mouth firmly fucking shut.'

Jack has a face like a Halloween cake, and his lousy breath had nothing on his body odour.

Luca bawls at him, 'Where's Julia?'

'Are you worried about her, would you like to see her?'

Luca spears him a glare, 'If you've harmed her, I'll kill you.'

Jack, bending down close, laughs in Luca's face, 'Of course you will.'

Luca's eyes fill with rage as Jack produces a syringe and jabs the needle into Luca's thigh. Looking down at Luca, Jack's eyes narrow to crinkled slits. Laughing he leaves the room, without another word.

Luca howls at him, 'You won't get away with this Mason, I'll have you, believe me.'

As the door shuts, the room becomes black again. Rolling across the floor, he looks for something sharp to cut him free, before the drug works its way into his system.

CHAPTER 53

Entering Luca's office at 11.05 pm, Rick finds the room empty. After having a brief look around the station, he asks the desk Sergeant if Luca's left the station. The Sergeant tells him he's not seen Luca since he came in. But he hadn't signed out. Leaving by the main entrance, Rick enters the car park to find Luca's car missing. Re-entering the station, he finds Sam sitting at her desk, staring at CCTV footage, 'Have you seen the boss?'

'No, the last time I saw him was about half nine, sitting in his office looking at some photographs, stretched out across his desk.'

'He's not in the building and his car's gone.'

'Has he signed out?'

'No, that's the strange thing, and Pete on the desk didn't see him leave.'

Picking up her phone, she calls Luca's mobile. The mobile goes straight to answerphone. Pressing the tracking app on her phone, it shows him leaving the station at 9.41 pm.

'It looked like when he left here, the tracker shows him heading towards Sloane Square, then down the Kings Road, making a left turn into Wandsworth Bridge Road. He then turned right into Carnwarth Road, and that's it. He must have then turned off his phone.'

Rick looks at Sam with a concerned look on his face, 'I don't like this Sam, something's amiss here. He wouldn't just leave like that.'

Sam snatches her keys from the desk, 'Come on; let's get down there.'

Running from the station, they get into Sam's car and roar off into the night.

Driving along Kings Road, Rick asks Sam. 'Did you hear about the murder in Clapham today?'

'No, I take its nothing to do with our three girls?'

'Doesn't look like it.'

'Who told you?'

'Davy Paton, do you remember him from Hendon?'

Sam smiles, 'Yes I do, he could talk the clothes off a Nun.'

Rick laughs, yes that's our Davy.'

He adds, 'They found the girl's body with her face bashed to a pulp, and her skull crushed. Her killer set her alight, trying to get rid of the body. They found her clothes nearby, torn to shreds.'

Sam enquires, 'Where did they find her?'

'At the back of council flats in Acre Lane, Brixton.'

'What is going on, things are getting so bad. I'd hate to bring kids into this world.'

Rick looks over and grins, 'Has it crossed your mind then Sam?' She doesn't answer.

Passing through the World's End district of Chelsea, Rick asks, 'Did you know the boss lived in the area where we're going as a kid?'

'No, I didn't.'

'The curious thing is, Albert Mason and his family also lived around there. In those days, it was a tough area. I knew of the area but seldom ventured over there. I remember once going there as a boy; it wasn't a good experience. We played football against Langford Road School; they kicked us all over the place, we were black and blue. And that was just their parents.' Sam throws her head back and laughs.

At the end of Wandsworth Bridge Road, they turn

right, into Carnwarth Road. Stopping halfway down on the left-hand side, opposite a block of council flats, they get out of the car and scan the surrounding area. The road's wrapped in darkness, except for the weak moonlight shining on the slated roofs.

Looking down at her phone, she tells Rick, 'He turned his phone off, somewhere here.'

To their left is a piece of boarded up land and a private car park. Spotting a small dark path between the two, Rick shines his torch in the path's direction, they look at each other and walk towards it. The sky above them is like a black lagoon. Tiny pinpoints of silver stars penetrating it. Halfway down the precarious path, they hear the river Thames, slapping against the embankment wall. Passing a green wire fence on their left, they stop at the river's edge. The Thames is stretching out like a broad black ribbon in front, and a fine mist is creeping towards them from the Wandsworth side of the river. With the bank on their right cut away. A large black silhouetted tree is leaning out over the river, looking like it's trying to reach over to the other side. To the left, peering through the old green wire fence, they can see old warehouses and other buildings in the distance. Shining the torch along the fence Rick spots a gap, 'Come on then, do you care for a midnight stroll?'

Struggling through the wire fence, they stand in the weighty blackness of the night. The large derelict site spreads out before them, and a warm breeze blows the aroma of wood smoke and river water in their direction. Entering the site, Rick points out the decaying houses on their right-hand side. Above the properties, distant street lights are casting an orange glow on the horizon. The houses look like nothing more than a ghostlike outline of some previous world. Now standing outside the properties, they can see the houses were abandoned many years before. A stiff summer breeze causes an old swing to sway unsteadily outside one house, its rusted chains creaking. Some houses had caved in on themselves, like a sponge taken out of the oven too soon. With roof tiles ripped off in places, they could see the wooden skeleton of the rafters beneath.

Entering the first house, dust is laying on every surface like dirty snow. Slivers of light shining in from the outside, show old cobwebs billowing in the draft. Rick thinks to himself, 'How long had it been since the house heard the laughter of children? How long had it been since it felt a coat of fresh paint or contained the aroma of Sunday roast dinner?'

It's a crumbled beauty of an era long past. After searching the ruins, they discover the only occupants are pigeons, spiders and bats.

On leaving the house Sam points her torch over to the left-hand side, 'Rick, look over there.'

The beam is shining onto large green gates. On reaching the gates, Rick pulls them apart, and they pass through. Only once they were on the other side, they could see the full size of the immense site which lays in front. What once was a thriving dockyard, is now a wasteland. In the distance, the moonlight is shining on two large buildings to their left.

Sauntering towards the smaller of the buildings, a sense of excitement stirs in the pit of Rick's stomach, as he scans the windows for any sign of movement within. Darkness gains upon them like a black wall, as clouds diminish the moonlight and stars above them.

Overgrown branches enveloped by a green tangle of rampant ivy are covering the entrance, as if warning them off. The reception area which was once something marvelled at is now a sorry sight of collapsed splintered beams and thick layers of suffocating dust.

In the reception area, they find the doors ripped off, lying on cracked marble floors. The graffiti adorning the walls is almost an improvement. Most windows in the building are missing or smashed, leaving gaping holes for the wind and rain to rush in and out. The water stained walls look like scars upon their skin. Ivy has gnarled its way through the broken windows, tangling its way throughout the building. The doors not torn off, hang on their hinges at jaunty angles.

Searching the lower floors of the building the cobwebs are hanging loose around them; the shattered glass of the windows is sparkling in the torchlight on the dirty floor. In some rooms, sections of ceilings are hanging limp, with fragments of plaster lying damp over a long untrodden floor. The building is a mouldering heap bowing down to the elements. With their footsteps echoing on the bare floors, there's a flash of brown fur, as several rat's dive for cover and make Sam jump. Entering a huge room at the back of the building they find rusted machinery. But it's still looking somehow at home, within the building's vine-covered walls.

Sam looks over at Rick, 'What was that? I heard something.'

Holding his breath with an audible heartbeat, Rick listens in anticipation. In the dead silence of the night, he hears a muffled scream which sounded like it came from outside. Without a second thought, they run back through the reception area and out into the night and head towards the other building, looking for the source of the scream.

CHAPTER 54

When Luca wakes, he's not sure whether his eyes are open or not. Straining to open them with his fingers, he grasps the loose skin of his eyelids, but there's still a bottomless abyss of blackness in front of him. He realises his ankles are now free, but the rope is still binding his wrists. Standing he holds his secured hands up, out in front of him, acting like a lance, poking and feeling the blank dark space ahead of him. Taking three steps forward, he bumps into something he can only describe as flat and solid; it's a wall. With his eyes adjusting in the gloom, he can see on one side of the room the door is ajar. A chill run through his body when he sees a pair of eyes — flashing like lightning on a pitch black night, staring straight at him, through the crack of the door and its frame. Jack's face is like a slab of concrete, sunken eyes and a slit of a cruel mouth below his misshapen nose.
Luca can do little as Jack snarls and lurches forward punching him full in the face. Falling backwards, he slumps on his back into the dust. Jack, stooping forward, retying Luca's ankles together asks, 'So, do you want to see her?'

Julia's heart misses a beat when the door opens and sees Jack filling the doorway, holding a hunting knife. Forcing herself to her feet her instincts take over, throwing any object she can find at him. Filling with rage, he advances on her. Leaping across the room she grabs at a boarded window, trying to get out. But only cuts herself on the glass left in its broken frame. Her grip slips as her blood lubricates her hands, making it impossible to hold on to the frame.

Luca hears Julia screaming; her cries are like music to his ears. She's alive.

Jack pushes her into the room; Luca notices her skin is pallid and stretched over her stark bones. Her feet are bare and clothes ripped to pieces. With her face caked in blood, it makes her unrecognisable.

Grabbing her Jack leads her further into the room, one hand grasping her hair at the back, his other hand holding the glinting knife to her throat.

He roars at Luca, 'Shall I kill her now, do you want to watch?'

Hearing a shout in the distance, Jack stops in his tracks. Julia, screams at the top of her voice. Jack puts a hand over her mouth and drags her across the room. As he gets her to the door, kicking out she wedges her legs on either side of its frame and pushes back.

Jack, looking over his shoulder, sees Luca trying to unfasten himself, shouting at the top of his voice for help.

Releasing his grip on her, Julia falls to the floor with a hefty bump. From behind, grabbing her by the hair with his left hand, he swings his right fist in a sweeping movement, smashing it into the right-hand side of her jaw, knocking her out cold. Dragging her lifeless body through the doorway, he carries her deep into the dark abandoned building.

CHAPTER
55

Against the night sky, all Rick can see is the crumbling walls that were nothing more than a ghostly silhouette of some previous existence. Shining their torches, they see crusty speckles of paint lining the floor with dust and the corpses of long dead creatures. Moving deeper into the building billowing cobwebs are brushing their faces.

Sam, putting her hand on Rick's arm, stops him in his tracks, 'Listen, I heard something.'
Standing still not moving, they stare at each other. Out of the silence a shout of a man echo's, from a dark passage leading off the reception area. There was something in the shout like there was pain behind it. The place seemed more like a long-abandoned prison or mental asylum, rather than an old commercial building. The building is a warren of corridors and staircases. Adding to the creepiness are green glow in the dark exit signs radiating off in the distance from the torch lights. They're about to move into the dark passage when they hear what they think is a child crying in the distance, but realise it's the whining of rusty door hinges somewhere in the building. Moving into the passage they hear the shout again, ahead of them.

Sam tells Rick, 'I'm sure it came from the left, further down.'

Rick stops outside a large brown door and puts his ear flat against it. Taking a step back, he kicks it with the sole and heel of his right foot, causing the wooden door jamb to splinter into pieces. Entering the room, he spots Luca in the room's corner, prostrate and bound. Etched with fatigue, Luca's looking like profound hopelessness is dominating him.

'It looks like someone's set your face alight and put it out with a shovel, boss.'

As Luca's getting to his feet, Sam asks, 'Have you located Jack Mason?'

'Yes, and he's got Julia, come on we've got to move.'

Scrambling into the corridor, they shine their torches for clues of Jack's whereabouts, Luca tells them, 'You two take the upstairs, I'll take the lower floors and the basement.'

Rick, points his torch at the rickety staircase to the right. They ascend its wooden steps. Sweeping ever upwards, the smooth dusty bannister supported with ornate wrought iron balustrades, guides them to the top. On reaching the summit, Rick whispers in his mobile for backup.

CHAPTER 56

Luca's lungs and heart are pumping, but the air in the basement doesn't seem to be enough, as his exhausted limbs slowly move forward. His footsteps are echoing through the dark, dank, cobbled corridor. In the distance, he can hear the faint sound of water dripping from an old pipe and splashing onto the floor. Inching along in complete darkness without being able to see a thing in front of him, he creeps through the battered skeleton of the dead building.

The corridors had been constructed in a way that his footsteps seemed to come from behind him. They also seem to take one more step, than he does when he stops. With his eyes slightly adjusting to the darkness, to his right-hand side he sees a tunnel entrance. Entering the tunnel, he spots a door on his left covered in moss. It has a brass coloured lock and doorknob, dulled with age. Its four carved panels giving it depth and texture. It's square-shaped and its sides are glowing with a pale light, turning the handle, pushing the door, just enough to see some light through the crack. Gradually putting his head through the gap, out of the corner of his eye he sees something coming towards him. Trying to jump back out of the way, it's too late. The pain is unbearable, as he collapses to the ground.

CHAPTER
57

Regaining consciousness two minutes later. He takes his mobile from his pocket and phones Rick, but realises there's no signal. Re-entering the tunnel, he heads back to the passageway. Turning right, heading further east. Fifty yards down, he comes to another tunnel curling away into infinite blackness. Entering the claustrophobic dank, river-smelling darkness. He hears the loud sucking noise of the River Thames against the wall to his right. Shining his torch in front of him, he sees two sets of footprints on the wet floor. Streaming through the tunnel wind is scattering pieces of tattered paper, sending them twirling into the air. The once beautiful arched brick walls are covered in graffiti. The floor littered with hypodermic needles.

  Without warning a heinous laugh, rebounds off the crumbling walls, causing him to stop and hold his breath. Moving forward further down the tunnel, a light in the distance casts an ominous glow in front of him.
Further into the tunnel, he notices a slight rise in the ground beneath him. He's meandering down the narrow path when he sees side passages branching off on both sides. Their destinations unknown. All the side paths appear the same as the main tunnel, murky and menacing.
Hearing distant whispers, he quickens his pace. His heart beating harder and faster, his adrenaline levels rising. Coming to the end of the tunnel the soft moonlight is setting the end of the tunnel aglow.
Exiting the tunnel, he finds himself on the bank of the Thames, short of Wandsworth Bridge.

Running over a steep rocky slope, he loses his footing and is sent tumbling.

Getting to his feet, his mobile rings, it's Rick, 'Hi Boss, we've got him.'

'Got who?'

'Jack Mason, we've got him cuffed. Back up as arrived.'

'Have you got Julia.'

'No, she wasn't with him, and he's not saying a thing,'

'Well, who the fuck have I been chasing for the last half an hour?'

He adds, 'Get to the river bank at Wandsworth Bridge as soon as you can, I'll meet you there.'

Continuing over the rocky embankment the river is flowing swift and strong. Scanning the embankment wall, the moon is finding every glowing angle. Continuing towards the bridge, he spots a figure dragging something over a wall, on the left side of the bank.

Climbing over the brick wall, he finds himself in a car park. In the shadows he spots Rick, and shouts over to him, 'Rick, I'm over here, quick. Did you see anyone coming out onto Carnwarth Road?'

'No, not a soul.'

'I know he's here somewhere.'

'Who.'

'I don't fucking know, but I've been chasing him for the last half an hour.'

Rick tells Luca, 'I'll look on the left, you take the right-hand side.'

The tarmacked car park is occupied by a few cars, wheelie bins and two builder's skips. Luca's approaching a skip when he's knocked off his feet by a towering figure of a man pushing past him. Getting to his feet, he sees the man racing across the tarmac.

Rick, hearing the commotion, spots the man heading his way. The man doesn't see Rick in time and runs full into Ricks right fist. Hitting the floor, he tries to get to his feet but Rick punches him again, this time to the side of his head. The tall, dark figure of the man covers his face with his forearms, cradling himself in the fetal position. Rushing over, Luca straddles the man, who's now lying face down. Grabbing him by his collar, turning the man, Luca's stunned. The man lying on the ground is Albert Mason.

Luca yells, spit flying into Albert's face. Holding his fist above Albert's face, he screams, 'Where is she?'

Grinning, Albert says nothing. Luca, raising his fist, is about to punch Albert in the face when Rick grabs his arm, 'No, Boss.'

Standing, Luca tells Rick, 'Watch him, don't let him move.'

Walking back to the where Albert sprang from, he pulls out the green bins. Sending them spinning across the tarmac. Tears fill his eyes when he sees Julia, prostrate on the floor, her face and head caked in blood. Bending down he cradles her in his arms. Reaching for his mobile, he calls for an ambulance.

Rick, hearing Luca talking to the emergency services, calls over, 'Boss, is she ok?'

'She's in a mess, but she's breathing.'

Within minutes, two ambulances and three police cars, scream into the car park.

With the Paramedics attending to Julia. Luca rushes over to confront Albert, 'You scumbag, I will make sure you go down for life.'

Albert laughs, 'You mug. You didn't have a clue. We even knew that skinny freak Reg was in the park that night, listening to us. I knew he'd been following me for days.'

Luca rushes at him, but is stopped by an officer attending the scene. Two other officers accompanied by Rick, bundle Albert into the back of the Police van. Rick slams the door shut, and the van pulls off, heading for the station.

Rick asks Luca, 'Do you want me to come to the hospital with you?'

'No, I'm fine, get back to the station. I'll talk to you later.'

CHAPTER
58

Martina and Franco enter the Chelsea and Westminster Hospital at 5 am. Reaching the ward, they find Luca sitting at Julia's bedside.

With tears streaming from her eyes, Martina whispers, 'Will she be ok?'

'The doctor told earlier; she will be fine after some rest. Her injuries are superficial, except for a broken nose. They're keeping her in for two days. Where are the girls?'

'I called Maria; she came straight over to my place and is with them now.'

'I can't wait for them to see Julia.'

Franco adds, 'How long has she been asleep?'

'Over two hours, she's exhausted.'

Putting a hand on Luca's shoulder, Franco tells him, 'The thing about life is, it pushes you until you break. To see if you can put yourself back together. I can see you are both broken, now you need to put your lives together again.'

Luca looks at Franco, and touches his hand, 'You're spot on, brother.'

With Julia still sound asleep, Martina and Franco leave the hospital. Martina, going back to the girls at her flat, Franco direct to the restaurant.

Leaving Julia sleeping, Luca takes a walk to get his head together. Exiting onto the Fulham Road, the clouds are rolling back and the morning sun is bringing the city alive. The streets are moving with a great river of people, red buses and black cabs. Over the last twelve months, his life had been in a void. A never-ending dark abyss, devouring everything around him. He knew all along he still loved her and knew he would come running if she ever needed him. They say pain dulls over time and things will get better, but it never has. No one had replaced her and no one ever could.

Walking through Elm Park Gardens, there's a chill in the air bringing the first hint of autumn. The trees are a riot of colour and leaves are pirouetting through the air, littering the pavement. Bathing it in dark red and brown.

Sitting on a bench in the square, he thinks about the future. His father once told him, yesterday is history, tomorrow is a mystery and today? Today is the present. It's the first time in months he feels positive about the future. As the trees stir above him, he has that wonderful feeling of going
home. He knows things need to change and they will start today.

Re-entering the ward, he sees Julia sitting upright in the bed, holding a cup of tea.

'How long have you been awake?'

'About twenty minutes, where have you been?'

'For a walk to clear my head. How are you feeling, you look dreadful?'

'Oh, thanks.' She says smiling, 'Are the girls ok?'

'Yes, they're fine, Martina has them at her place.'

'I want to see them as soon as I can.'

'I'll bring them here after they finish school this afternoon.'

'I can't wait. I've missed them so much. You too.'

Seeing her eyes filling with tears, he hugs her and tears drip from her cheeks on to his white shirt. With his big arms encircling her frail body, she feels protected and safe for the first time in months.

She doesn't want the moment to end and tells him, 'I love you, Luca Rossi.'

CHAPTER
59

The beach at Positano is a blaze of coloured parasols. With golden sand covering the shore, way out into the distance, a gentle sea breeze is slicing through the air, giving a refreshing coolness to the otherwise warm weather. Visiting Positano, his father's birthplace had always been Luca's dream. With its vertiginous houses tumbling down to the sea in a cascade of sun-bleached peach, pink and terracotta. And its steep streets, flanked with wisteria-draped hotels, Luca couldn't be happier. Watching Amalee and Darcy playing on the beach in front of him, he feels like he's in heaven.

Watching Julia sitting on the beach, the beautiful blue ocean's waves are crashing onto the sand. It's now four weeks since he got her back. Now fully physically recovered, the previous day she told him she couldn't stop thinking about what she had gone through. She likened it to a horror movie playing over in her head. Attempting to analyse what she had gone through, made her see it all over again. As if her brain was unwilling to let the horrors go.

Against the percussion of the waves is laughter, coming in bursts, rolling like the ocean. He can see Julia's golden hair blowing in the breeze, and her youthful face turned toward the sun. When they were apart, his heartache was like something eating at his chest, tearing its way to his heart. His despair had rung him out until he was dry inside, and no more tears would come.

Laying back on the sand in the glorious sun, he lets his new found happiness soak into his bones. He wants the feeling to be there still when they were both old and grey. He knew love was when your heart melts at the sight of someone when you feel lightheaded and free. When you ache to be with them, to look at them, to touch them, that is love. As he closes his eyes and savours the moment, his thoughts shatter when Amalee and Darcy run across the sand screaming with delight. And jump all over him, 'Can we have an ice cream please daddy.'

The End

Printed in Great Britain
by Amazon